LOST
in Oklahoma

D1519518

A WORK OF FICTION BY
SHIRLEY MOORE

to Barbara
Best wishes. Hope you enjoy!

Shirley Moore

Cover photography by
Lori Root, Rootsquared Photography
www.facebook.com/rootsquaredphotography

Edited by Jacque Ramirez and Layne Moore
Book layout by Layne Moore

Printed in the United States of America

First Printing, 2016

ISBN-13: 978-1536997620
ISBN-10: 1536997625

This is a work of fiction. Names, characters, businesses, places, events and incidents are either the products of the author's imagination or used in a fictitious manner. Any resemblance to actual persons, living or dead, or actual events is purely coincidental.

For the eyes of the Lord are over the righteous,
and His ears are open unto their prayers:
but the face of the Lord is against
them that do evil.

1 PETER 3:12 (KJV)

Chapter 1

It all started the day my brother decided to drive to California to see his daughter, son-in-law, and family. Phil would drive his second car first to Enid, Oklahoma to pick up his wife, Frankie, who was working in the Enid hospital. They would then drive to California in their new Buick.

The plan was to take me with him from Arkansas City and have me drive their second car back home to Arkansas City. It all seemed so simple at the time and I was glad to help out with his vacation plan. Nothing daunted Phil, and his plans always worked out wonderfully.

Arkansas City sits on the southern border of Kansas. To the south is the beautiful State of Oklahoma and directly on the border is Chilocco Indian School. Our day started early and weather-wise was perfect for travel.

Usually when Phil visited California he flew by plane, but this time he wanted to take the long, leisurely drive and visit a few tourist sites on the way. I helped them stow all their luggage in the new Buick and we ate a quick breakfast so they could get started on their vacation.

Phil wished me a safe trip home and said a quick blessing for both of us as we traveled in different directions - me driving home northeastward and Phil and Frankie starting their long trip west. Good brother that he is, he first pointed out my road as I started the motor and gave me directions back to the interstate highway, which I thought was very thoughtful of him. He also had filled the gas tank full again, then we all had a quick goodbye hug.

We started off in different directions then it hit me. I was all alone and traveling home in a strange car I had never driven before.

I assured myself the car was fairly new, in good shape and filled with gas.

It was bright daylight and I was not too far from home as I zoomed out toward the interstate. Thirty minutes later, I realized I had missed the turn off to the interstate and was on a secondary Oklahoma road which was going east, but not northeast.

Where was I going? Surely there would be a turn off this minor road back onto the big interstate highway soon. I kept plugging along mile after mile after mile and there was no town, not even a farmhouse. *Where had I got myself?*

It was kind of funny. I went barreling on down the highway hoping to see a sign announcing a crossroad or a town. Nothing! The road seemed to go on forever and I was just looking for some sign of life but not even so much as a cow appeared.

Plenty of crows, however, and hope spring eternal. Maybe around the next bend a town or a farm would appear. The Cimarron River suddenly appeared and I wished it had read *Arkansas River* instead. I needed to get to a civilized town for something to eat and drink. Thirst was driving me on.

Kingfisher the sign said!! We hadn't come through a town with that name on the way down to Enid, Oklahoma from Kansas. I needed to get an Oklahoma map from some place and a cup of coffee to quench my thirst.

First stop was a diner. Then second stop was the Kingfisher Bank for money, which was running low in my wallet. At first when we started to travel I thought twenty dollars would be enough. Now that I had taken the wrong turn and traveled south instead of north, I might need some more for gas.

How far south is Kingfisher, anyway? And please help me turn around and go north, Lord, toward home. I kept talking to the Lord and a quick prayer for guidance never hurt, I thought. *It worked, so now I'm headed right.*

The Kingfisher Bank appeared before the coffee shop on the corner at the right side of my way A good parking place was near the door, very handy for me. I needed to get a little cash out of my ATM bank account in Ark City for extra gas and a meal, then zoom north toward home.

Maybe the bank would have an Oklahoma map available for lost travelers from Kansas. It wouldn't hurt to ask for one, I reasoned to myself.

I opened the car door but it was rudely slammed shut before I could even move. Someone opened the other door and slid into the seat beside me. The back door opened and a man climbed into the rear seat.

I felt pressure at the base of my skull, like hard metal. The female voice beside me said, "Drive south, quickly!"

I was too scared to look around. "Are you going to kill me?" I asked shaken and stunned.

The voice beside me answered, "Not if you do what I want you to. Quickly pull out and turn south!"

I got the message and my teeth chattered so loudly I couldn't speak, but I knew enough to obey. They had taken me prisoner in my own vehicle and as it was two against one, they had all the power. I could kiss Kansas goodbye, because the highway went south.

My whole life was going south now and my plans were all in shambles. I might never see home again. My mind raced, *where had I gone wrong?* Just one little mistake and here I was a hostage. Nothing seemed fair about this deal anyway.

I was too scared to ask any questions, but I quickly figured out they had just robbed the Kingfisher Bank, and I was helping them escape. Even if they let me go, the Kingfisher Police were going to believe I helped rob the bank of, I didn't even know how much money. I would eventually end up in an Oklahoma prison somewhere.

Tears started rolling silently down my face. It's a good thing I don't wear powder and rouge. My tears practically washed my face as I thought of the injustice of being locked up in prison for a crime I didn't commit.

Chapter 2

Silence prevailed. They didn't talk and I couldn't say a word either. On we rode, mile after mile. *Where did they want to go? Why didn't they take my car and leave me in Kingfisher? Why, why? Questions raced through my mind. Were they serial killers or just bank robbers?* My mind was racing through a lot of scenarios.

The first, being my body dumped in some Oklahoma lake and forgotten forever and never found. Prison even looked better to me than this!

A big hat covered the female's face entirely and I couldn't see sideways any features of my captor's face. I didn't dare turn around to look at the man in the back seat because I knew he didn't want me to see his face either. The brief glimpse of a ski mask at first sight of him had scared me spit-less anyway.

They could hold me for ransom in some dark cellar cage, but nobody in my family had any money to buy my freedom. Then again, I was a worthless package. I couldn't see any good out come from this situation for me.

My mind raced like a squirrel in a turning cage! *What could I do to escape? What could I do to them when we got where they wanted to be? What would they end up doing to me then?*

No answer came to illuminate my frantic thoughts. El Reno loomed ahead. *Was this the place they were heading for? Would they need to stop? Were they part of a gang of outlaw thugs, or acting on their own?*

On we traveled past more contented cows just standing free on lush fields of green grass. A sign loomed up – *North Canadian River*! I began to shake. *Well, if they wanted to dump me, here was their chance. Just heave me off the bridge into the North Canadian.*

I only hoped they wouldn't shoot me first. Fatigue was taking over and I could barely think of a plan. Driving was never my lot, as I usually rode as a passenger when traveling.

Driving was very tiring in a way. Staring at the road became hypnotizing after several hours of continued staring at a line. I thought my bladder might burst, but finally the woman ordered a bathroom break. We stopped at a park rest stop and she accompanied me into the woman's bathroom building.

She kept her hand in a jacket pocket pointed at me. The place seemed isolated and no one else was in the cement building. There were rows of stalls for elimination for traveler's use. It smelled!! I needed a restroom break, so I hurried ahead of her and squatted over a stool, because I wasn't gonna touch it with a ten-foot pole. She kept her face covered mostly and didn't face me squarely. Quickly opening the door, she motioned me outside ahead of her.

He waited for us by the door and when she pushed me out of the outhouse he had his black stocking cap mask back on his face.

"Hurry up," he growled at her, "We haven't got all day!"

He shoved me toward the car doors which stood open, both front and back tailgate, as she darted back inside the cement restroom for women. He pushed me in the front driver's seat then shut the door, but went back to the car trunk door to slam it shut.

I grabbed the extra set of car keys from under the front seat, jammed them in the ignition, turned the motor on and took off with the back tailgate door still flopped open. He was hopping mad and chased me clear up to the highway, but I was in high gear and running, gunning the car engine for dear life! And, my dear life outran him off down the highway.

I didn't care which way I drove, just any direction to get away from those two crazies. Going deeper into southern Oklahoma was safer than submitting to two crazy bank robbers. My only hope was they would not grab another unsuspecting motorist and come chasing me down the highway!

It looked as if God had answered my prayers for safety and truly helped me survive this day! Now, if He will point me the right way north for home. This became my mantra.

I started looking for road signs to determine how far south we had driven from the Kingfisher Bank. Also checked on the gas gauge to see how much was left. I was really hungry and thirsty, but didn't know how far some food might be, or the next town or gas station. I didn't want to be found by my captors again either, because I figured they would be twice as mean when, or if, they ever caught up with me again.

There was a sign up ahead, I hoped it would say food. It said, *Chickasha Highway 81. Chickasha. The name of an Oklahoma Indian tribe...maybe,* I thought.

I needed to keep the gas tank filled to the top level even if it wasn't yet down below the half-way mark, so maybe a stop at the next town past Chickasha for gas was a good idea. I still felt the awful presence of those two crazy bank robbers sitting in my own space!

The quiet drone of the car motor, and the scenery passing by, soothed my spirit a little bit. I began to feel safer as each mile rolled by. The feeling of being freed from a certain death sentence was so joyful, I almost had to sing praises aloud.

My plan was to stop at the next town's police station to report the bank robbery and my escape from the two felons. Hunger was my first priority as it invaded my thoughts. A good meal and an Oklahoma map, then report to the police.

I rolled through the Wichita mountain scenery and Paul's Valley wondering who the "Paul" was that had a valley named after him. Finally a gas station loomed up and I turned in to top off the car tank. Maybe they had maps there, so I went to ask, and what luck, there were all kinds of good candy bars at the register too! Everything I needed and maps.

I resisted the urge to warn the store attendant of my escape from the bank robbers because I was afraid he would think I was a nut-case. Most folks would have found the story not only to be crazy but my escape to be unlikely.

Still if the robbers got up this far from that rest stop, the attendant would likely be in danger, as twenty miles was not very far away. This would be a likely place to stop.

I felt I had to warn him in a non-committal way so, as I opened the door to leave, I casually remarked I had heard of a Kingfisher Bank robbery and the two felons were headed this way.

"Be careful." was my parting advice.

He just smiled like he thought it was a joke and waved a hand. I slammed and locked the car doors then opened the Oklahoma state map to see where I was. When a car passed by on the highway, I started shaking again, but it was just a big friendly trucker. Next town the map said was Duncan.

Chapter 3

When my brother and sister-in-law got home from California, they were going to wonder about all the mileage I put on their car. But what a story I would have to tell them about my adventure!

I ate four candy bars over the drive to Duncan, Oklahoma, so I decided to stop at the police station first before dinner and alert them to the danger that might be headed their way. Police stations are always plainly marked and easy to find in smaller town. So I just followed my instinct and sighted police cars parked in front of a large imposing building just off Main Street.

What a welcome sight! I stowed all four candy bar wrappers in a waste basket near the building and entered the police station property. Two busy folks on phones looked up to see me as I entered and leaned up against a glass window. *What should I say to begin?*

"I need to report a bank robbery," was what I actually said to the face behind the glass window. They directed me into a little office room off the main reception area and a couple of officers listened with polite interest to my horrible experience about the Kingfisher Bank.

Yes, they had been advised of this shortly before my arrival and they were very interested in my part in the whole affair. One question they didn't understand was why I happened to be parked in front of the Kingfisher Bank at just the appropriate time? Did the two bank robbers have any connection to, or knowledge of, me?

"No way! Absolutely not!" I gave them my driver's license to verify my story. "I told you, I parked there to withdraw money from my bank account from my Arkansas City bank, because I was a long way from home and getting hungry."

Second question, "How could I get lost when I was so close to the Kansas Oklahoma state line? In Enid?"

It did seem funny that I appeared to be so dim-witted, I thought to myself. "I did have the presence of mind to escape from the kidnappers," I informed the two officers.

They were making fun of me and apologized. They had already called my bank in Ark City while we visited and knew quite a bit about my sterling reputation. They advised me of the best eating place in Duncan and, trying to make amends, they actually asked if I wanted an escort to the highway back north toward Kansas.

"No way, Officer. I'm afraid I would be accosted by those two felons if I took the same Highway 81 back north. I'm going to try and find the interstate highway back north. Surely there is a safer way to head north so I won't have to back track on Highway 81."

The policemen told me they had squad cars going north on 81 Highway and planned to locate them if they came this way. I couldn't identify any faces out of their felon file because their faces were either covered by a ski mask or veiled by sunglasses and hat.

"They probably will cut off through farm fields and avoid the highway," One policeman said. "If that would make you feel safer."

"Their body build was just normal and they looked fit enough to hike through any terrain," I said. "All-in-all, my experience in traveling Oklahoma highways has not been pleasant today plus, I'm hungry and it's way past noon. Breakfast was at 5:00 a.m. in Enid."

"Come on, we will treat you to lunch at the best place in Oklahoma to show our hospitality." The Sargent in charge said.

Off we went on foot to "Jack's Luncheon." The place was filled with a gang of bikers touring Oklahoma parks and lots of fine hungry family folks too. Everyone seemed pleased with smiles, just talking and eating.

One family rose and left a large five dollar tip for the table service, I noticed. So the meal must have pleased them. We sat at their table which was quickly cleared and sprayed clean with a good smelling soap, disinfectant, I suppose. The waitress brought water and menus quickly then left us to read and decide.

My nerves began to relax and settle down. I told the police Sargent thank you for being so kind and hospitable.

He just grinned and said "We want you to think well of Oklahoma, our State, and plan to visit us folks again."

I replied, "I guess I just ran into the worst kind of you folks."

The bikers sitting at the next table heard us talking about the best way to traverse Oklahoma and came over to get acquainted.

"We heard you had a bad intro to our beautiful state and we would like to give you a better tour with our group of bikers."

They saw I was interested in their travel plans and the whole idea of cycles traveling together. Such a novel idea, and economical, too. They gave me a quick lesson.

"We are traveling families on tour of this great state and we stop and stay at the best scenic views each day. It's a relaxing way to travel with all your gear packed in a tiny vehicle and gas mileage is awesome! It's comfortable if you have the right head gear, too. This biker bunch likes to take one vacation each year together because we have been friends a long time – from grade school on up."

"It sounds mighty tempting, but no thanks. I've never owned a motorcycle or even ridden on one in my whole entire life. You guys have to know a lot more how to handle your cycle wings than just driving a car." I said.

"Oh we understand and wouldn't expect you to want to ride anything but your car and we could just ride along as your escort, but you would have to stay with us as we visit all the best places around the state."

It seemed like everyone in Duncan had heard of my fate pretty quick until the biker told me they had a special radio CB station for police news that warned travelers of things like bad weather, tornadoes, flooded roads, and dangers anywhere in the vicinity. Just the thing people needed to be safe as they traveled.

"Marvelous!" I exclaimed.

They also knew about the bank robbery while I was still being held hostage. Of course, they all wanted to come over and congratulate me for escaping. I felt almost like a celebrity. We visited a long time and they showed me their itinerary. They knew who I was the minute the Duncan police chief and deputy escorted me into Jack's Diner.

"Come on outside," one biker by the name of Jonesy said. "And I'll show you my wing, my pride and joy."

He spoke of his wing like it was near to his heart and his wife confirmed my idea. She said he took care of it like it was family. Maybe spent a lot of time on it too.

"Oh well," she said, "We women have our hair-dos and new duds too. I can't explain our hobbies."

We traipsed outside and examined the bike. It looked very sturdy, big and hard to handle. But it had plenty of room for his wife to ride along also.

"You are very accomplished to be able to handle this bike!" I said.

"Oh, come on. Anyone can learn to ride a bike – hop on and I'll give you a spin."

Before I could sputter, "No way!" someone lifted me on the bike behind Jonsey and off we went! Was I going to risk my life again after just regaining it? Wow, me without a helmet but, just around two blocks. What a smooth ride! In a few seconds we were back in front of the restaurant where I quickly hopped off and thanked Jonsey.

Mary Jo, his wife, handed me a map of their ten day itinerary and planned vacation that included park rest stops, plans for each site to see and enjoy, even a historical explanation of each location.

Someone in this bunch is a history teacher, I thought to myself, *and has done a lot of background state study to compile this itinerary. Their ride has a real purpose of knowledge and fun both put together.*

I was really impressed and interested. Someone in this bunch had to do some real research and love teaching Oklahoma history to get this trip together.

"I might ride along a little ways following your group to that first place you are going to camp. It looks very interesting and I've never been there before. The details of history are very interesting too."

A one day vacation in Oklahoma wouldn't be much, but it could be fun to visit. Maybe I should enjoy just one interesting site in my neighbor state before heading home. I had actually been bored with nothing to do until my brother, Phil asked me to bring his second car back to Ark City from Enid last week.

The bikers had instant CB radio communication with the Oklahoma State Police and could garner any news pertaining to the Kingfisher Bank robbery situation. They were always kept abreast of new developments concerning weather as they travelled also. It seemed they were very well protected in every way as they sped along the highways and checked out the scenery. Protecting me would just be another act of Oklahoma hospitality.

Wow, I thought, *no other state has people with such warm concern!*

Shirley Moore

Chapter 4

The bikers were taking a quick walk through Duncan's main street to visit stores for food supplies and anything they needed for the next day. I used the time to visit the bank for funds for another day of travel and rest my body from being cramped up in the car and driving so long.

My stroll led me to the end of Main Street where a man was feeding animals in an outdoor cage; a bunch of dogs, cats, and whatever else wandered into town. He picked up one pup and started petting it, then hugged it close to his heart.

"Is that your special friend?" I asked.

"No," He looked at me sorrowfully. "I'm going to have to put her down. Today is her last meal." He actually had tears in his eyes.

"Why?" I asked. "You can't mean that, surely?"

"Yes. Her time's up now and it's the law. Only so many months is allotted for each one to be fed."

Such a sorrowful look was in his eyes I couldn't help myself. "Let me hold her, will you?" I looked in her dark brown eyes and the little dachshund actually kissed me on my cheek. "Why can't you give her to me," I said in a flash. "What is the cost to free a doggy from the pound?"

"She has had her rabies shots and is spayed but we don't charge for that," the attendant said.

"Well, I want her and I'll buy one of your little carrying cages now and pay whatever it costs. I need a little companion."

The deal was made and he even threw in her little dark blue blanket. I handed him a $100 check for a donation to help feed the other animals.

"What's her name?" I asked. "And what is your name, too? We should get acquainted because I'm taking her back to Kansas."

"I'm Bill Akers, ma'am, and the pleasure is all mine. You have made my day brighter by giving Benny Jo a good home. Thank you again."

All our paperwork concluded as he handed me Benny Jo's medical file and I hefted up the cage and blanket. He also supplied a collar with medical tags attached describing her shots. Oklahoma takes care of everybody well.

Benny Jo went along willingly in her new little collar and lead chain like she knew I had just saved her life. We had become instant pals. Finding Benny Jo was better than anything I had ever imagined. She, of course, had to check me out first before giving me her total love because being in a dog pound had been a strange situation. She didn't really know what kind of personality I had: mean or loving. I guess she was just glad to get out of the wire compound not knowing her time had almost been up.

What a horrible thought, *if I hadn't gotten lost and come on down to the Duncan dog pound today, Benny Jo wouldn't have been here for me to save.* One good thing that has happened out of this whole 'lost day' of my Oklahoma fiasco.

I reasoned since the Lord had spared my life, I could do this for Benny Jo and give her another chance. When I got back to my car, all the bikers wanted to pet Benny Jo. When I told them about this almost being her last day, they really thought this was another miracle that had happened to me. First escaping from the bank robbers and now saving Benny Jo's life.

I needed to buy a bag of dog food to take along and dog bed for the pup, so into the store I went. The dog had to stay in the car, but she settled right down on my car pillow to rest just like it belonged to her. What I didn't realize was Benny Jo was training me and it took a while before I caught on.

We humans think we are training our pet companions but it's really the other way around if we are kind and loving. We provide the best care for our little animal friends. When I returned to the car, Benny Jo sniffed the package of dog food to see if it was her favorite brand, and it was, thanks to the advice Bill Akers had given. Bill informed me if I had bought the wrong brand of dog food, Benny Jo would have gone on a hunger strike for a week and practically starved herself to death before she would lower herself to eat.

What determination I thought! *I had a lot to learn. How would we get along?* I wondered if all breeds of dogs were so picky or if this was just a dachshund trait?

The bikers and I all gathered in the City Square Park for instructions on the highway ride. Four wings in the lead, my car next, and the other four wings in the rear. They would take turns and reverse formation at times.

If anyone needed a bathroom break before each alternate town stop, they had a signal. Each one had the CB radio to make sure everything was copacetic.

Is there a bond between bikers? You bet! Aside from each one desiring the same brand of bike, this bunch had grown up together in one special hometown: Miami, Oklahoma right on the eastern Kansas Oklahoma line. The bikers would eventually end up there at the end of their tour.

I put all these thoughts through my mind. *If I stayed with the bikers on the ride I would eventually end up in Miami, Oklahoma which was straight east and only a little ways south of the Kansas border. Arkansas City was right straight west and sat on the border right in the middle of the Kansas State. I could get home without too much trouble from Miami, Oklahoma.*

With a bunch of friends like these, the bank robbers would never want to see me again, and I wouldn't feel so alone traveling Oklahoma parks with Benny Jo and my biker friends.

Everyone, including me, had purchased things they needed at the local Walmart. I had a package of underwear, socks, plus two T-shirts, and walking shorts, extra dog food, toothbrush and paste. Also I had my ever present package of Snickers bars to munch on while traveling. I'll bet everyone has his little munchie packed. I even saw jellybeans in more than one biker's hand, so I didn't feel guilty with my candy stash!

There was one thing the Duncan Police Chief hadn't counted on. Much to their dismay, the biker's had drawn a Duncan paper reporter to Jack's luncheon and he got the full news of the King-fisher bank robbery and kidnapping. The pictures we took made every Oklahoma newspaper in the state and now, the bank robbers knew who to follow with lots of travel plans the bikers had provided.

This news was not going to be good when they realized their plans were available to the robbers by way of the newspaper article. Something else bothered the Duncan policemen: what if the felons wanted to get revenge on that poor Kansas woman who had outsmarted them? She left them at a park rest stop in the middle of nowhere without transportation. Because of this news story, she might be in more dangerous trouble than she knew.

Of course, the reporter was only doing his job and he never would have thought he was aiding and abetting the two felons. A juicy piece of news, with two interesting twists, had elevated his story state-wide and nobody could miss it, especially those interested in knowing the bikers travel plans.

Reporters never think of who they are helping commit the crimes with all kinds of information given. Even the biker's itinerary!

The Duncan Police Chief quickly radioed this news to the bikers on the CB radios because they needed to be alerted to possible dangers! You never know what goes through a mind that turns to mischief with a gun.

Not only was the story picked up state-wide, but it was nationwide news the next day, reaching as far as California. When Suzanne's brother, Phil, read the California Riverside News, he was totally shaken up and wondered how this was all happening. Had his sister totally lost her mind?

Phil immediately tried to call on her cell phone. He needed to understand what was happening and how she got so far lost and how she was captured! Nothing made sense to him. Was everything alright now and was she headed home? He had thought he never had a worry in his mind until he read the Riverside newspaper!

Nobody answered his phone's ring yet. Frustrated, he decided to call the Duncan Police Captain for news, to get to the bottom of all this mess. What he heard from the Duncan Police Captain made his worry increase.

Because of the newspaper account, the bank robbers now knew exactly where his sister was each day. They were all alerted to the danger inherent upon them but due to the fact that no one knew what the two desperados looked like, they could approach as perfectly innocent strangers and strike back where no one would suspect.

"However," the captain added. "I have told all of the bikers and your sister to be suspicious of anyone approaching them now, and the eight bikers are pretty well able to take care of themselves. Plus the dog is alongside your sister at all times."

"What dog are you talking about?" Phil was totally puzzled.

"The little dachshund dog she rescued from the Duncan Dog Pound now travels with her," Captain Hayes replied.

The mystery seemed to be getting deeper and deeper, so Phil thanked Captain Hayes and hung up totally confused. It seemed to him, although she had been in deep trouble, at least now she was relatively safe. But he still wanted to hear her voice personally to hear what she had to say.

Suzanne was thinking, *maybe I should travel on alone home after this first park stop because I was only bringing more danger to the folks on their bikes. They needed a peaceful vacation, after all and they didn't need to travel with my problems added on.*

"I ought to be able to drive back home without getting lost again," she reasoned aloud.

When she voiced these doubts they all assured her they weren't worried and that she should enjoy the park they were headed for. It was full of horseback riding, fishing, and trails to walk, with beautiful scenery.

The wives were all talking over the plans of food and entertainment for each day at the park. Everyone wanted to hike the trails on foot for exercise although biking was fun, hiking was healthy and that stirred up the blood and brains too. These folks were into health as well as fun. They enjoyed a great camaraderie together.

The horse stables were a great lure for a change of transportation. Some of the bikers already knew how to ride horses while the others were all willing and interested to learn. Swimming and canoeing were well looked forward to. These folks were willing to enjoy and venture anything.

Jonsey even joked he would be open to ballooning sometime in his future. Oh the joking comments on that idea were funny to Suzanne!

Ray asked, "How were you going to put your bike in the balloon basket, and did you have a specific color balloon in mind so we could wave at you as he flew over?

Jonsey took all this joking in great stride and commented, "As I flew over the camp I might poke a hole in the black cloud to rain down on your heads."

It all sounded like so much fun to Suzanne she really wanted to see this great park they were all talking about. Even tenting there would be comfortable, for everyone had planned well for this park. Of course, the van would be a well-protected place for her pallet and then for Benny Jo's little bed. She would have to learn how to cook over an open fire too, but she didn't worry about it too much. The canned supplies they had brought could be eaten cold or hot and still taste good. The bikers were hospitable enough to share their food with her.

They did not want to alarm Suzanne, but they had all agreed among themselves to be real alert and careful of any strangers showing up or acting different around their group.

Suzanne had described every detail from her memory about the Kingfisher bank robbers' voices and mannerisms. Dictation and word phrasing seemed important to Ellen, one biker's wife, who might have been an English major.

Shirley Moore

The two felons were considering their plight of being left afoot at the park rest stop. The only information they had on the woman in the car was the Kansas license plate number and the make and model of the car. They had never thought in their wildest dreams that she might escape from their clutches. But what Suzanne didn't yet know was he had hidden the bank bag containing the stolen money in the car wheel space.

Bart decided they must hike over from farmlands to a safe place before nightfall, if possible, and make plans to track her down somewhere, somehow? He wasn't sure how he was going to find her car, but he would never stop looking for it, and she would probably never find the hidden moneybags anyway. He decided he would have to just find a way to identify her by the car tag number and he needed to go to the county clerk's office to do that.

What a sad mess they had found themselves in and it did not sweeten his temper. Already his girl, Patty was blaming him for being stupid and careless. He thought about dumping her as she was just extra baggage anyway.

Patty always thought she was the brains for all of their plans, but actually she was just as careless as he was about everything. Thinking and planning was always left up to him. Patty would never have thought to rob a bank for money in the first place. She was just drifting along depending on others to provide for her and she never contributed anything. She was just plain lazy!

The more he thought about this, the more he wanted to just dump her somewhere else! And, because his patience was running thin, he was close to boiling over at Patty's constant nagging. Bart never confided his plans with anyone and definitely not with Patty.

He wasn't even sure where the county courthouse was, but he took out his map to calculate where they were and where they needed to go for information.

The money he carried in his pocket would not last long, and if he had to keep feeding Patty it would disappear faster. The town closest was Rush Springs, a far hike but doable. They must be in Grady County, but where would the courthouse be? Bart called an old friend to come and pick them up from out in the boondocks so he could get a second wind and some information. Bart and Patty were both totally exhausted from the very start of their most exhilarating, exciting adventure.

Bart called his old friend, Tobi, who had the getaway car they left in Kingfisher by mistake, and begged a ride home. The reason they had taken the wrong car was never brought up. It was just a stupid mistake no one had planned on. The one thing Bart could never do was admit he had made a mistake. It was always just a bad outcome to be blamed on circumstances. Of course, it was always a good way to keep anyone from blame.

The newspaper in Lawton gave Bart all the information he needed to track the Kansas woman's car down. Maybe he could get lucky and get in the wheel well without alerting anyone if they were all asleep.

First off he had to get rid of Patty and convince her to stay in Lawton alone. He really didn't need someone dragging him down or hanging on and maybe messing up his plans to get the money-bags back.

Bart needed to borrow his old friend's car but didn't want to give him the real reason, which was to track that Kansas woman down. This was a job he needed to do alone without Patty or anyone else in his face giving advice. He would rent a vehicle but would really rather not turn loose of any of the stolen money if he didn't have to.

Bart was trying to figure out a way to use everyone else to his advantage. It seemed he needed a vehicle to get to Warika Park immediately to put his plan into action! Plan one: ditch Patty, borrow car, hightail it to Warika Park! Maybe he needed to pay a little money to his friend to borrow the car. It wouldn't hurt to ask anyway and offer a little cash for a day loan.

Money always sweetened the deal, Bart thought! *People listen when money talked.*

Tobi didn't listen or fall for the extra money offer. His car was not for hire to anyone without him in it, as the car was his only good possession. Bart was not that reliable as a friend either and Tobi was still wondering why Bart and Patty were walking back in the boondocks of Oklahoma?

No information changed hands and no one had offered thanks or gratitude to an old friend for their rescue either. The old friend became wary of this new request even if payment was dangled in front of him. Maybe it was time to back away.

Tobi reasoned he needed time to think about it. Bart was in a hurry to get away to pick up some transportation from somewhere. Bart began to mull over in his mind what other vehicle he might acquire cheaply. A moped was one thought. A bicycle was his last idea. Bicycles took too much energy, plus were never fast in a getaway situation. It was a pity that his bicycle was the only thing he totally owned.

Duncan, Oklahoma was quite the historic little town, Suzanne read in her brochure of Duncan facts. The little restaurant boasted many facts in this brochure to prove how proud they were of Duncan history.

Being part of the Chisholm Trail US Highway 81 from Texas to Abilene, Kansas was a big plus in this brochure. She really began to wonder about all these Indian tribes who settled in Oklahoma. In her brochure 36 tribes were listed.

Patty had tears in her eyes when Bart told her she had to stay home in Lawton while he left on business. She didn't quiet down until he pulled out $300 to keep her happy while he was gone. He didn't plan on coming back and he had purchased a small moped by secondhand that he hoped would not give him too much trouble to get to Warika Park.

That took his account down some bucks and he really needed to get that Kansas car fast to replenish his wallet! The gas mileage for the moped bike would be a lot less than a car, so he guessed he was better off than if Tobi had let him borrow his car.

Shedding Patty made him feel fifty pounds lighter and fancy free. Bart now felt he could accomplish anything he tried alone and on his own. The Duncan Police Captain alerted the Warika Police of the situation he thought needed their attention.

If the bank robbers intended to harm the Kansas woman by following her to the Warika Oklahoma State Park, the police might survey all who enter the park for awhile just to be careful. No one wanted any harm done in any Oklahoma state park. The one drawback was, no one knew what the felons looked like.

The only description was they were both of young age and very fit. No car could be described by the Warika State Park officials who were also put on guard of a possible mal content person headed their way. Only people who seemed curious about the bikers and their companion from Kansas would be looked upon as a person of interest.

Chapter 6

Suzanne finally plugged in her travel phone and called Phil to explain how she got turned around the wrong way at the Enid turnpike, heading south instead of north.

"Don't interrupt me until I finish my explanation Phil," Suzanne said. He was used to her way of talking and shut up quietly. "First I ended up in Kingfisher which is several miles south of Enid. I was hungry and stopped at the bank in Kingfisher for money in case I needed more food or gas. I parked at the convenient place right in front of the bank." She went on and on through the frightful ride until her escape. "Please forgive me," she sobbed.

Phil was so glad everything turned out okay, he just couldn't be mad. He assured Suzanne he would continue his vacation as planned and hoped she would get home safely. Everyone needed a little vacation time now and then.

At least he wanted to have her check in every so often so he could be sure. In his mind, he hoped nothing else could go wrong with eight biker families accompanying his sis. As he thought about what she had told him, he reasoned the felons would not want to be anywhere near her ever again if they had all that money in their possession.

She was completely safe now, so why were the Duncan Police so concerned? Phil called the Duncan Police Captain again.

His first question was, "Why would the felons even want to bother with Suzanne again if they were free and have the bank's money?"

"I have to admit we have not completely searched her car underneath and thoroughly as he should have," replied the Captain.

The reason he wanted to keep her under continued surveillance was to be sure the money wasn't stashed somewhere he hadn't looked. It was a good way to entice the felons if they were following any leftover bank money in the car and a good way to catch them.

Phil was really upset that the Oklahoma Police would use his sister as a lure to catch a hardened criminal without even warning her.

"She really would never know how to deal with or even recognize someone bent on harming her. She never carried a gun and wouldn't know how to shoot it if she had one," he explained.

The only consolation he had was the knowledge the eight biker families were on the alert for the felons. It comforted him to know Suzanne had a little dog along with her. He was going to talk with Suzanne and warn her of the ways to be careful every day now.

The bikers were not stupid either. They all knew their motorcycles were prime targets and were never left unattended by at least one couple each day of their travel. Guard duty was a given. Each couple took their turns guarding all the cycles as the group enjoyed each pleasure the parks offered.

The cycles wings were treated like family and never neglected. Especially now, that they had been cautioned about possible theft.

Benny Jo just settled down comfortably. She never let Suzanne out of her sight because the lady was now family in her heart and she knew good souls when she saw one. Good food, her favorite brand, was offered twice each day and a clean dish of fresh water was always available. What more could a dog want?

Well, Benny Jo wanted lots of love and she got lots of love and attention from all the motorcycle people, as well as Suzanne. Her little dog heart grew more content every day and the great outdoor park was good to sniff around in.

Each day was a miracle of discovery for Benny Jo too as the whole world opened up to her. However, she never forgot her main instinct to be guard dog of the camp! This was her main way to be important to all the people: guard dog duty, day and night.

Benny Jo was the first one to notice the man on the minibike who rode past their camping spot in the Warika Park. The dog was curious as the strange moped slowly putted past their car the second time, then turned around to head deeper into the wooded area off the road in the back of the biker's space.

Benny Jo had a curious nature and watched everyone and everything she saw to learn about people, all types of people. She traveled a circular route several times each day and night winding around their camping space. She had to be sure nothing crossed the perimeter unobserved or undetected by her. Benny Jo barked loudly if any animal ventured into this circumference she secured for the motorcycle camp.

Suzanne always praised the dog on every occasion even if it proved to be a false alarm by some little possum. Sometimes a good-looking meaty bone was presented to the dog for the special bravery of routing a raccoon out of the camp.

Racoons can be notorious for raiding trash cans in every Oklahoma camping area where they always dug litter loose and trashed the whole camp at night. Benny Jo delighted in chasing and scaring them away. Anyway, she felt her guard dog duty was appreciated.

Setting up camp tents and one stove for meals was not hard to do because it was a familiar chore everyone had accomplished many times before. Their camp was made secure wagon train style that night.

The campers relived and remembered many other good trips and recalled many funny events to delight Suzanne about their wanderings and inexperience when they first started traveling by bike. They had each learned many things to avoid from their past trips.

But this trip was a first with car and dog rescued from the dog pound and a bank robbery to boot. It was something they had that was unique about this trip. One trip to the Grand Canyon in Arizona, they remembered, their bikes were taboo and they either walked or rode mules down to the bottom of the canyon. One had the wrong kind of shoes on, lost his toenails and had to be helicoptered out of the canyon at great expense and greater pain.

They all had learned many painful lessons in funny ways at times. Inexperience was blamed for all of the bad times but everyone helped out when someone needed extra kind, loving attention. It was thought staying close to home and seeing sites and parks in the home state might be safer to do this year but no one had counted on a bank robbery to put them on their guard. It was good to sharpen their wits and remind them to always be watchful and careful no matter which state they traveled.

Carol and Dave drew first guard duty 10:30 to 1:30. Second guard duty was Kate and Jim: 1:30 to 4:30 a.m. Guard duty people didn't have to do any cooking the next day but were royally fed and treated.

Guard duty was over for the week then all the events could be tried out. The helpful watchful nature of their plans always provided a secure feeling of carefulness in their camp. One of the motorcycle crew families was a state trooper and kept contact with his local patrol officer.

This personal contact made the group feel more secure about their travels in state. Each one felt more confident because of this knowledge - maybe a little over confident. Danny, the vacationing state trooper, felt the extra burden he carried but did not complain. He just became a little more cautious and alert. He watched the dog circle their camp three times each day and really approved of the little critter! It helped guard duty too, much to his amusement.

Danny made special friends with Benny Jo, their helpful watch dog. He felt he owed her special attention because of her loyalty to the group. Benny Jo lapped up all of Danny's attention too. The truth about traveling camp style is to make yourself as comfortable as possible with mosquito spray and lotions against all kinds of bugs, if possible, while enjoying the bugs natural habitat twenty four hours each day. Oh, the wonders of Warika Park beckoned and half the fun was planning each day of their stay.

Relating to each adventure, everyone in the group had found some special thing to enjoy and part of the fun was to share these things with the rest of the group.

Their first meal over their campsite was hamburgers, of course, along with chips and dips. Lots of lettuce, tomatoes, onions, and pickles, fruit and cookies alongside of canned pop or tea on ice.

Suzanne had nothing to labor over for shelter like the tenters did. Her little van provided instant perfect protection from cold or rain, her own little cocoon. Their little campfire made everything seem cozy and comfortable. Most of the bikers used pallets for beds. Everyone wanted to explore the camp as much as possible and try fishing as well as exploring or hiking or on horseback along the trails.

Jonsey and Mary Jo volunteered to be campside watchers first day out of the goodness of their hearts. Jonsey could fish nearby or Mary read a book in camp and snack on cookies.

Bart was being eaten alive by mosquitos but he had brought bug spray along to keep this from happening. Bart was no novice to outdoor Oklahoma living so he knew what the necessities were for comfort. He just hadn't had time to spray himself for protection from those little blood suckers. His meager food supply was just what he was able to sling in his back pack along with his bug spray: baloney, bread, cheese, and mustard. Yuck three times a day! Well, he hoped it would only be one or two days at most.

The one drawback he hadn't counted on was the stupid little dachshund dog that always gave him the evil-eyed look every time he ventured past the bikers' campsite. Whatever spying he had to do would be on foot maybe at night.

Did they ever leave their campsite unattended or would he have to wait until the woman traveled on alone, he wondered.

Bart was smart enough to know he shouldn't get friendly with any of the bikers and especially not the women. There was a very good possibility she would recognize his voice even though she never had seen his face. So he could never strike up a conversation with any of her companions. Bart was smart enough to know he must remain incognito, to be undetected. He was bone tired after riding the little moped all those long miles from Lawton to Warika Park. Every bone in his body demanded rest.

The only thing he was interested in was the woman's car and he hoped they might all go off and leave it unattended at some unguarded moment. Bart did not relish the thought he might have to follow the woman clear up to her home town of Arkansas City either. He would keep the car under surveillance at all times.

The nights did cool down after the sun went down. Bart decided to take a long afternoon sleep so he could prowl around the camp at night after everyone else had settled down. He could quietly case the camp and see if it would be guarded at night.

Of course, the dog was a very real set back he hadn't counted on. Dogs always were alert day or night and barked! Bart wished he had some poison to feed the dog but had not planned that far ahead. Maybe a strong sleeping drug would be better.

Bart carried drugs along with him. Wherever he went, a small dose of sleeping pills went with him. He quit taking the pills to save for the dog thinking this would make it easier for him to get into the van's wheel case. That dog must be silenced!

After a long nap Bart woke up about midnight then decided it would be a good time to survey the biker's camp. He had not decided yet when to entice the dog with a doctored up hotdog or how to do it incognito. The camp was well guarded and lit with a small flash lantern which he decided was extra trouble but far enough away from the car tailgate not to be too much of a hindrance.

He really could not get in the wheel well while the woman and dog were sleeping next to it, so he would need to plan a daylight distraction so he could draw them all away from the car.

A daylight distraction that could draw everyone just a little way away what could he plan? Bart wished to know a way to get a park ranger uniform, but discarded that idea quickly as being quirky.

The idea of becoming a bonafide park ranger employed to empty trash cans also went through his mind, but that would entail real work and use up all of his daylight hours to boot. His mind raced over a lot of useless ideas and he was becoming discouraged a little bit. He decided to doctor up a piece of bologna and leave it on the perimeter of the biker's camp just a little off the path hoping the smell of meat would distract the dog enough for a quick look into the car.

He kept hoping the woman would go off hiking or swimming with the group to get her away from the van. As far as he could determine the group had plans to do something of interest each day and he was trying to figure out a way to listen in on their plans.

The smell of cooking meat made Bart really hungry. While he had very little provision, even the bones tossed to the dog made him hungry as he watched the little mutt chomp on them. He needed to replenish his supply of food because his canned goods had run out the second day after he arrived at the park.

Suzanne went to take a shower at the public bath house with Mary Jo and Julia. A Warika State Trooper came by the camp to visit with the crew and assured everyone they were going to be checking up on the campsite regularly to ensure their safety.

Suzanne wasn't there to ask him any questions and none of the bike families wondered why there was any surveillance of the group. They were just glad to have the patrol watching over them.

The trooper didn't offer an explanation of why he was assigned their camp care. Danny came over to identify himself to the Warika trooper and they wandered down the road a little to converse over the matter.

However the Warika State Trooper didn't mention anything about the money or bank robbery. No one had advised him of why the money hadn't turned up yet either.

His instructions were to notify headquarters of any strangers approaching the group and quickly turn pictures and information over to the headquarters for examination of anyone who approached the group. He figured out who they were looking for but his hope was for peace without gun play.

If anyone strange seemed to be casing the camp the trooper would be sure to spot them. Danny was glad the police wanted to keep his group protected. He began to go over all the information he had in his mind trying to reason it all out.

Revenge seemed to be a good possibility but you would have to factor in personality and temperament of the felons and that was impossible for him to do. Danny discussed his thoughts with the other guys.

Art, Bill and Neal were not the suspicious type and all thought the felons had long gone happy to be alone with their stash. Most of the guys were not the suspicious type like Danny, Jonsey and Dean.

Danny didn't want to ruin their vacation with his troubling thoughts so he cooled his comments from then on and just let everyone enjoy Warika Park and their vacation time. Danny could visit with the park patrol and get updated reports on police information whenever he got curious.

Fishing and swimming were going to take up a lot of their time along with horseback riding and hiking the trails. Sunshine, sunshine, sunshine rewarded them each day.

Danny also made sure Suzanne had a camera with her and was ready to take pictures of any strange people who came near her or paused at their camp. Suzanne had relaxed her vigilance a bit now, however, and she didn't feel threatened because she had lots of friends camping alongside her van. Nothing out of the ordinary happened.

As one day passed into another peaceful day, the gang's planned activities and entertainment wiped away all the bad experiences of her past days. Their third day at the campsite, Benny Jo seemed to sleep a lot and take extra naps and she wondered a little bit about this unusual behavior.

Judy said, "You know cats sleep most of the day and run around the house at night. Maybe Benny Jo is a nocturnal dog who does that."

"I don't think so," Suzanne hesitated. "Benny Jo seemed more wide awake during the day than she is now."

This began to worry Suzanne but she left the dog to guard their camp with Judy and Neal. The group was going trail hiking and Benny Jo was so lethargic, Suzanne decided to leave her in the camp.

It took twelve hours for the drug to wear off. Benny Jo had eaten at 9:00 p.m. the day before as she circled the camp with dog guard duty. When she finally woke up, the hiking group had long been gone but Judy and Neal were guarding the camp. Judy told Neal to fish if he wanted to and she would guard camp awhile.

The stream was close by and it was so peaceful. Even if she snoozed or napped a bit she would still have the dog for guard duty. It seemed the little mutt preferred the company of the women over the men, which was funny. Judy decided not to take an afternoon nap, but to read and stay alert.

Anyway, Neal was within hollering distance and she could see him as he cast his line and walked up and down the shore. Every day had been peaceful since they arrived at Warika and no one had showed up to arouse their suspicion.

The flies, mosquitoes, and bugs had been their only annoyances. Judy sprayed Benny Jo and herself with bug repellent. The dog tolerated it but didn't understand or like it and planned to wash it off as soon as she got down to the lake. It was just another human quirk she found puzzling.

The other puzzling quirk was why anyone would leave a good piece of meat on a paper plate outside in the bushes by their campground. Benny Jo planned to look and see if this would happen again.

Suzanne never had placed any food outside the camp to tempt any animals and the raccoons would surely be scouring the trash barrels eating anything they could find left alone outside. It would be a race between the raccoons, squirrels, and the dog to find any meat left again.

Her long sleep had rested her and she couldn't quite understand why she had been so tired. The group walking along the trails enjoyed the clean fresh air. They had prepared themselves against the flying insects. Their tennis shoes were most comfortable for footwear also. Just make sure not to step on a sleeping snake.

"Do snakes sleep on rocks to sun themselves?" Suzanne asked.

"Oh yes, water moccasins as well as rattlesnakes do," was the reply. That gave everyone a bit to think on.

"What about spiders?" Suzanne asked.

"Oh, there are millions of them overhead in the trees, you can see them by flashlights at night and with their red eyes lighted up," Ellen said. "It's a fascinating sight in the nature study program offered here each week."

This information was very unsettling. With millions of little red-eyed spiders living overhead in the trees and snakes napping underfoot or gliding along riverbanks, what was she doing invading their domain? No one else seemed bothered by all this information, so Suzanne decided to cool it.

Actually when she thought about it, she lived on a pile of bugs at home. Ants, bees, roaches, mice that she knew about and probably black snakes, lurked about close by to feed on the mice. If we had to share the planet we must make the best of it was her conclusion. Onward and upward! The nature walk was very satisfying and very few had injuries by twisting ankles on rocks or tripping over tree roots.

Suzanne was carefully cautious because caution had become second nature to her since her kidnapping adventure in Kingfisher. Each new person was viewed with a microscopic eye just like a bug. When they finally arrived back at camp, she was glad to discover Benny Jo was her old self again, floppy-eared and smoochy. The long nap seemed to rejuvenate all her doggy energy.

Lunch was coming up next for the group and the cooking smelled good. Everyone had a good appetite after their five mile hike and each one felt better because of their exercise. The only thing Suzanne didn't like, was knowing how hundreds of little red-eyed spiders shared the park with humans.

"Sometimes," she said. "A little information was too much knowledge." Everyone laughed because they all knew Suzanne was talking about the spiders in the trees.

If Neal had caught any fish he didn't bring them home because he was adverse against cleaning them. No one in the group asked him how his fishing was because they all knew what he would say. Judy never covered for him or offered to clean his fish either. Neal and Judy had to listen to all the hiker's adventures. They sounded great, so Judy and Neal planned to take the hike the next morning. Jim and Kate had camp site duty the next day.

The planned lunch menu was simple because steak, salad, and baked potatoes was for supper that evening. A little swimming and rock climbing would be enjoyed as well.

Most of the group wanted to try canoeing and waterskiing. They did not have a boat for that stunt however and Suzanne was glad. She did not want any accidents to happen to those happy dare devils.

Horseback riding was going to be a big adventure for her. Dean and Lila were the horse experts in the group, having been raised on a farm all their lives.

Maybe if they could find one old nag she would ride with them on their next horseback adventure. Sleep would come early for her the first day because the hike took a lot of her energy and 5:00 a.m. was powerful early that day.

She did not want to be a wet blanket on their vacation days so she kept quiet about any spider fears. Swimming would be very relaxing, Suzanne decided then she would take Benny Jo on a hike around the park campsites. Maybe see who was close to their camp and check out all the neighbors.

The swimming was very relaxing and really gave her muscles a good workout. No one had the energy or inclination to join her on the walk around campsites, however. Suzanne and Benny Jo were on their own. As she checked out, she told the group she would only be gone up to one hour. That was all the energy she had left but she promised to help cook their supper that evening.

Bart had left the park to visit a store for more food supplies. It seemed that this project was not going to be as easy as he had thought.

Finding the right time to pilfer the car and dope the dog with sleeping pills was going to be a major task. He decided he should not poison the dog because that would be a very suspicious and damning act. His grocery supplies had all run out so he had to back track a little and replenish his supplies. Not only did he have to watch out for the dog, he had the cycle group to contend with.

Bart wondered if he would be better off to wait until the woman went home to Arkansas City. He wondered if the money would be safe if left in her car that long. Problems, problems!

Bart and Patty had made a strategic mistake when they had kidnapped the woman outside of the Kingfisher Bank. Their plan had been to be picked up by Tobi as they exited the bank with whatever money had been gathered. However, scanning for surveillance cameras carefully, Tobi was slow in driving up to the bank to meet them and the Kansas woman had arrived at the door exactly as they exited with their loot.

Tobi was frustrated that this mistake had happened and he had not been in place as planned. He could not really blame anyone for this error in timing and he was glad they had not harmed that Kansas woman. He was really mad once he reasoned out why Bart was so insistent on following her in Warika Park.

Tobi was money-wise and even though Bart had not confided in him about his mistake, he began to put two and two together. It was a very stunning revelation for Tobi to think about why Bart would not let him drive the car to Warika. The money!!

Bart was planning to retrieve the money hidden in the van and disappear with all of it!! Patty and Tobi were left out and dumped. Bart was going on alone and cutting Tobi and Patty completely out.

The more he thought the madder he got!! Well he could get up to Warika on his own and the newspaper kept him informed of all the biker's itinerary. Look out Bart and Warika!

Tobi packed a few supplies mostly food and bug spray along with a sleeping bag to sleep in the car if he needed to stay overnight. He could just about envision Bart's face when he arrived at the park; that little punk had a good scare coming to him. Tobi didn't want extra baggage along with him, so he slipped out of town quietly alone. It was dark but he knew the way to Warika Park and he had prepared well for this day.

Bart was going to be surprised when he showed up. If the plan wasn't to Tobi's liking he would put a stop to it. Bart didn't know everything there was to know and Tobi was going to give him a few clues. This caper had three people start in together and there would be three to finish it together...or else!

It would be best to keep a cool head and go into Warika Park as a friend to Bart. Just give him time to make up some insane excuse of why he went to the park alone and didn't explain to Patty and Tobi what extra plans he had going.

Tobi was well aware of Bart's temper and didn't want to alarm him into a temper tantrum. "Keep cool" was his motto and control over the situation. When you had to deal with a childish idiot you had to give him a little room to squirm around in.

Arriving in his car with a few extra provisions, Bart should welcome him and not be too suspicious. Maybe he would come clean and explain why he was at Warika and welcome a little extra help from Tobi. Then again, maybe not.

While he drove all those thoughts were going through his mind. It was a good way to keep awake on the drive. His car was making good time and good mileage. It was a very good thing he had not parted with his car and let Bart travel on alone to Warika, because Bart might not have planned to ever return it again. What a thought!

Now he was getting suspicious again! But, that was how their friendship began. Bart needed friends who could supply him with things he needed and Tobi owned the getaway car they should have used in the Kingfisher Bank heist.

While the plan had been well thought out, Bart had jumped the gun and used the Kansas woman's car instead of waiting for Tobi as they had planned. Patty had to obey that crazy fools reasoning and change of plans at the last minute! When would they ever learn!

Bart was like a ticking time bomb, always ready to go off! Emotionally he was immature to Tobi's way of thinking and Patty was only interested in having a good time with plenty of money to spend. She wasn't any better than Bart in brains, but she was not a ticking time bomb ready to go off at any second. The turn off sign to Warika Park loomed ahead. At last he was near…now to find Bart's campsite.

Tobi didn't really know how Bart had traveled to the park, but Patty had told him about a moped being considered and how Bart had to leave her in Lawton for lack of room on it.

A moped! What a dolt Bart was! When you thought about it, maybe he was just being conservative, especially if he had lost control of the money bags. This was another disturbing conclusion. If Bart had lost control of the bank money, who had the dough? It sure wasn't Patty or she would have spent it already. So to Tobi's way of reasoning the money would still be stashed in the Kansas woman's car.

No wonder, Bart was being cagy. He didn't want Tobi to find out how dumb he had been. It made sense now and Tobi intended to help Bart and bolster him up. Tobi began slowly driving through the park looking first for a moped. It was after dusk and he had to scout closely.

Locating the cycle group was easy because they had lots of space, but Bart was hidden so cleverly he was hard to find. Finally the second time around Tobi found the little squirt. He did not stop there, being cautious, he looked for a camp space a little way off from both of them.

Tobi would contact Bart on foot later or set up a meeting where they would not be observed. Carefulness was Tobi's first concern. Tobi also noted the biker's camp guards. He thought they would be taking extra care for their motor bikes, and not know of the hidden bank bags in the van. He thought to himself. *What a mess Bart had got himself into. What a mess.*

Supper was chili the second night at Warika Park and it sure smelled good. The bikers had brought nutritional drinks as well as tea, coffee, and pop. There was such a variety of fruit and drinks no one could complain. Fresh veggies were all on ice.

Art brought his harmonica to provide dinner music for the group and Valerie took everyone's pictures at the supper scene. "Oklahoma" show music was the favorite songs, because they all knew some of the words from the show. This was their state and they were proud to be Okies, cause Okies are okie dokie. Suzanne thought she couldn't argue with that. They were a fine group in her book.

She just kept quiet about her home state and enjoyed their loyalty. About 10:00 p.m. the group quieted down so as not to annoy other campers who might want to rise up early to fish at dawn.

Benny Jo made her last trip around their camp just to see if any raccoons were lurking. Nothing was there to disturb. She did smell another strange odor, something human.

Another new car had arrived that evening but nobody paid any attention because cars and campers were arriving and leaving at all times from their different sites.

Benny Jo liked all the activity going on. Then she decided to lie down in her little bed for the night. The campers decided they did not need night time surveillances for the camp and let their guard down a bit because of the police patrol in the park. Everyone began to feel more at ease and it was decided day patrol by one couple per day would be sufficient.

Tobi fixed his little campsite stove and tent by his table but he still planned on sleeping in his car. He decided to rest and relax awhile before hunting up Bart. In fact, it wouldn't hurt to let Bart find him at this camp site. It might give Bart something to wonder about too.

Tobi had not decided how he was going to play the scene out yet. He was not too eager to have his scene yet, because he really didn't know what was in Bart's mind. He ran off to Warika Park on a little moped bike when he could have included Tobi and Patty in the car. Maybe Bart was just ashamed for being so stupid.

Friends should trust friends when in trouble, Tobi reasoned.

He was also aware that Bart trusted nobody. This was why Tobi would not loan out his car. Patty was too trusting when she told Bart had given her a little cash then left town alone on a moped. The cooked camp meals all smelled good to Tobi and made him hungry. His supper was going to be very simple: ham and cheese sandwiches and pop.

Got to be ready for action when it comes time, he thought.

The whole camp ground quieted down for the night except for the hoot owls, police patrol and a few wakeful folks fishing or frogging quietly.

Suzanne was totally exhausted each day and really conked out on her pallet in the car. She put a little net to keep out bugs at the rear of the car.

Benny Jo took a bathroom break off in the weeds by the lake. The plans the group had discussed for next day were very interesting to Suzanne and she hoped to find an old nag to ride along with the group. Also planned was a trip to a nearby store for supplies. All the women enjoyed shopping in any kind of vacation store.

They were going to go to the museum and listen the next night to the spider oration from the naturalist at Warika Park. Suzanne called this nightmare night. When she told the group what she had called this nature talk night program they all laughed.

Jonsey kidded her as he spoke. "As long as you can't see all those little red-eyed spiders they won't bother you." Everybody laughed at her fears along with Jonsey.

Suzanne thought to herself, *just wait until we see all those million little red-eyed critters.* She kept quiet about this thought, however and did not want to spoil their anticipation for the science walk at night.

It was the only way they would know what bugs shared their outdoor park. Silence and quiet prevailed as everyone completed night time sleeping arrangements. Showers, bathroom breaks, and supper clean up over quietude prevailed. One lamp was left glowing at the midst of camp.

Chapter 7

Bart decided to sneak over to the motorcyclist camp just to see what kind of surveillance they used. His hopes got up when he saw their nighttime couple was not in place. They had lowered their guard a little because of Warika Park guard patrol. This suited Bart and he thought he might be able to drug the dog, but had not figured how to get the woman away from her car.

Bart listened and heard all of their plans for the natural science lecture and spider night time program next night. He wondered if they would leave anyone to guard camp during the program. He also wondered if the dog would actually be left to guard camp alone!

"No way," he decided. A little mutt dog would never be trusted that much! He decided it would be safe to case the car when everyone had gone to sleep.

If he could sneak up and peer into the car window without waking the dog or anyone else he might get brave enough to get the money out quickly and leave before waking the whole camp up. The question being was he quick enough to get the stash and get away before getting shot by the police patrol?

He could handle the dog, and maybe chloroform the woman, but what else he could think of to do? The fact that everyone was sleeping did help. All Bart lacked was cunning and courage. He did lack chloroform, however, as he had not planned this far ahead. Timing was everything!

Tobi finished his sandwich and chips then took a short stroll to the lake. It was very beautiful and peaceful at night and the stars overhead were all clearly visible to complete the picture. He wished their bank robbing plan had not gone so far astray The problem,

Tobi thought, was impulsive disobedience to the original getaway plan. It was time to walk over and talk to Bart to see if he was planning anything stupid again. Two heads were better than one, but Bart had never learned that. All of his last minute jerky decisions had brought on this disaster to their plans. Tobi went around the bend over to the cyclist's camp then back tracked on the trail to Bart's campsite. It was completely empty!

Bart had gone back for supplies and chloroform but Tobi had no way of knowing what Bart planned. He decided to wait quietly and see if Bart returned the next day. It was hard to figure out what was in Bart's mind, as he was nothing like Patty. She would have spilled all her beans by now. Bart had to be pried open before you knew his thoughts.

The camp had quieted down and Tobi watched as the park patrol slowly went by without disturbing any quiet. They were very silent and unobtrusive in their patrol. Tobi wondered if they wore night goggles to enhance their vision. He observed the little dog jump in the van and settle down for the night beside the woman.

Benny Jo's nose told her there were not hot dog treats tonight and the raccoons were not out and about yet to pilfer trash cans for left overs. Tobi decided to head for his car and retire. He hoped to elude all the bugs too.

Bart had gone back to purchase items he needed and the chloroform he thought he might need to use. His plan was not a sure thing yet and he needed to perfect it so it would be fool proof.

Was any idea ever foolproof? he wondered. The thought that he himself had screwed up the perfect plan for the Kingfisher Bank robbery still rankled him. He could not abide criticisms either. It was a weary task to go for supplies that he thought he needed.

It was a long weary ride for more supplies on his little moped minibike but the task had to be done! By the time he got back to Warilea Park he was very tired and just wanted to rest. It was necessary to check out the woman's camp and car and dog however-er.

So there is never any rest for us wicked folks, he thought.

He had not spotted Tobi's car or camp spot yet, but he did have to check on the money van just to be sure it was still there. Bart didn't know what plans the Harley motor cyclists had made for their day. He really needed to know every detail he could hear for his next plan.

Wearily he packed all his supplies in plastic bags tied shut to keep the raccoons out. It had been a long exhausting day for Bart and his strength needed to be replenished by a long rest.

Snoozing under a little tent underneath his cement camp table is where Tobi spotted him on the next trip around Warika Lake. Well if Bart was sleeping as heavily as his snoring sounded, he really needed the rest so Tobi didn't wake him. He planned on an early rise to come back for his visit. Maybe bring coffee and a little breakfast to create good will again. No bad accusations!

The biker's camp had a quiet peaceful night and it led them all to feel they had nothing to fear. So they began to be less careful of guard duty and depend more on the park police surveillance. Not everyone left the camp at the same time, however, so someone was usually fishing nearby or resting or cooking dinner at their camp via their schedule.

Tonight's supper would feature fried chicken, which was every-one's favorite, plus fresh vegetables and corn on the cob. Suzanne especially loved the corn on the cob dripping with butter and salt. She didn't even crave any dessert with this planned menu. It was easy to fix for the kitchen crew who drew duty.

It seemed to Suzanne every day was filled with perfect weather and they were favored with Oklahoma delights. The perfect sunset soothed her soul and it was just what she had needed - a perfect vacation day with good friends and plenty of exercise. It would be over too soon, but she planned on writing them and keeping contact with these special friends she had accidentally made. They were all smart, educated, and generous folks you could easily trust and emulate. They each had respect for one another and abided by that golden rule. Treat others with love and respect. No wonder they all got along so well with one another.

She sometimes wondered what had happened to the bank robber and his friend. She also wondered if it had been worth his effort to rob a bank in the first place. So much danger for little gain in wealth! Then you must hide all the rest of your life knowing you could be caught and imprisoned.

"Was that little bit of money worth it?" she wondered aloud as she talked to Benny Jo, her pet companion.

The Warika camp police were watching everyone closely as they registered and came in. They noted the two single men who were camped in different parts of the lake's camp but figured they had just come in to fish. Families came in to hike and ride horses and seek out nature trails together. Everyone had their own interests and no one looked alarming.

The Duncan Police Captain had not yet asked the camp police to search Suzanne's car because they were hoping the bank robber had left the money in the wheel well and would need to keep the car close by. The captain did not want to wait too long before he searched the car, but he wanted it searched while no one was watching.

What a bad situation to let the press give out the ideas and information to help the robbers and create this mess. All by himself he had made the most stupid blunder and set up a little unsuspecting Kansas woman as bait for two criminals to shadow. He must act quickly!

The Duncan Police Captain talked on the phone each day to the Kingfisher police captain and the Warika Police Patrol. He needed to learn what each thought about the bank robbers and if they had any suspicious characters under surveillance.

Suzanne's brother called her again and she assured him all was peaceful as far as she knew. She did agree that her treatment of getting away from the felons would have made them very volatile if they ever met up with her again.

Suzanne did not know very much about cars in general, and had never changed a flat tire in her entire life! She would not even know how to search a car for the loot. If it was not visible she would assume there was no place to hide a bank bag. Some women were savvier about hiding places but not his little unsuspecting sister. Phil wondered how careful she was now, and questioned her about the camp security.

Suzanne assured him the Warika patrol was superb, and camp patrol was tight because of the Harley's worth. There were eight couples to keep watch over everything. Since it had been so quiet for the group for several days, they felt the danger had passed with the felons long gone on another spree. The Duncan Police Captain was the only one who still had doubts about this theory.

Next day was horseback riding day and the group had scheduled an early morning ride. One couple agreed to abstain from the plans and do camp side watch, Bill and Valerie. They were ready to relax and enjoy a rest from the 5-mile hike of yesterday. Valerie hoped Benny Jo, the camp dog, would stay with them, because she was a good little mascot and would alert them to anything strange.

Benny Jo was awed by the big horses and thought they were some strange breed of dog. However, the horses ignored her so she was content to stay in camp. Benny Jo saw the people get on the animals backs and wondered at the power and strength of the strange critters. It was still so early the camp was not fully awake and everyone had a cold breakfast. Benny Jo munched her dog food contentedly.

Chapter 8

Tobi was pretending to be an early morning fisherman. He observed the group of bikers leaving on their horseback ride but also noted one couple was left guarding the campsite. He made a pot of coffee and decided to contact Bart and let him know he was here to help in whatever way he could. Tobi needed to find out for sure what Bart was up to. He hoped it was nothing ridiculous like revenge, but was unhappy with the thought it might be the car containing the bank loot.

The fact Bart had never mentioned money was disturbing in itself. He normally would have been bragging and gloating all over the place if everything was okay. Bart had an infantile mind and Patty was not too much more mature either. The smell of coffee awoke Bart as Tobi approached his homemade little campsite.

He sat up foggy in a daze as he gazed on Tobi and the coffee cup he held out. "Okay, out with it. What are you doing?" Bart asked very quietly.

"You seemed to need some help and a cup of java," Tobi said quietly.

"What are we doing here and why?" Tobi asked reasonably calm.

"I think I need a little vacation away from Patty."

Bart used this as an excuse instead of an outright lie. It was partially true. Patty got on everyone's nerves, Tobi knew, but he also knew there was more to be heard. He waited patiently as Bart drank the hot coffee gratefully. Maybe they could reestablish their trust in one another, Tobi hoped. He also knew he had to handle Bart with kid gloves because of his immaturity.

"I thought you might enjoy a little java to wake up this morn. It's still real early and most folks are still asleep. I'm camped a little way over in the next camp. Come on over and I'll cook breakfast," Tobi said quietly.

Bart was still being cagey and wary, wondering what was up Tobi's sleeve. Because he was untrustworthy himself, he couldn't trust anyone else either.

Poor sucker, Tobi thought to himself. *He is always unsure of himself, so he never trusted anyone else. What a clod!*

"If you had asked I would have driven you up here in my car." Tobi scolded Bart. Wrong thing to say, he saw immediately. Bart shut down totally miserable.

Being scolded for any reason mortified Bart and destroyed his sense of control. He did not know how to handle criticism and it crumpled his sense of worth. It was best for Tobi to be quiet and assuring at this point.

What little self-assurance Bart had was fading away and he could not acknowledge any failure on his part. He must brag and be capricious at all times, make fun of any errors and pretend to be all in control.

The coffee tasted good to Bart and the offer of food for his breakfast finally eased his distrust of his old friend. "I'm all out of sorts and kind of ragged, Tobi," Bart replied, "but breakfast sounds good."

Maybe I need a little help, Bart grudgingly thought.

Tobi won't be as condemning as Patty would have been, because men understood one another. Tobi never put Bart down or tried to destroy his ego of self-worth. Tobi was always the salt of the earth. Bart began to unwind and relax as he woke up.

"That coffee just hit the right spot." he muttered.

Tobi felt their relationship was better now. Bart only needed a strong shoulder to lean on and a good meal. Patty was the one who usually babied Bart, but she wasn't here so Tobi had to cook up a good breakfast of pancakes and sausage to get him started for the day. Tobi thought he ought to be able to handle that himself for once. Bart went back with Tobi to his campsite in the next quadrangle. The pancakes and sausage revived him along with the sugary syrup and more coffee.

The horseback riding adventure was sure different than Suzanne thought it would be. Everyone followed single file along the track and the horses were so well trained she thought just about anyone of any age would be safe on the trail. The ride was slow and pleasant so no one would fall off their horse unless they fell asleep. None of the horses offered to run off or buck anyone off. Suzanne felt quite safe and enjoyed the different scenes.

The only thing she had to remember was the horses were cross-trained, whatever that meant. If she pulled the reigns with her right hand the horse went left, then if she pulled the reigns with her left hand the horse went right.

It was a good thing the leader had explained it to her carefully because he saw right away some of the folks didn't understand cowboy language yet. When the group met at the five mile site there would be coffee and donuts served and a little water for the horses. She could almost feel like she was a real cowgirl. The sunrise was perfect in Suzanne's estimation along with the coffee and donuts.

This trip was well worth the price charged for the tour. The early hour was pleasant as Suzanne had always been an early riser. The group only had one grouch along on the ride. He kept everyone in stitches with his comments. Even he had to be awed at the beautiful sunrise.

The ranger warned everyone they might be a little sore when they got back to camp because they would use muscles they had never used before, even if the horses had done all the actual work and carried the burden.

Hanging on the carcass of a big horse took muscle power they had never used before. He warned them a good hot soak in a tub would be the only antidote to help their ailing back sides. Well, that was good for some but Suzanne didn't have a tub to soak in, just the showers in the restrooms.

Well, their pony ride tour guide was right. When they got back to campsite, Suzanne heard a lot of groaning as they dismounted. They thanked the horse trainer and told him this was the highlight of their trip. Suzanne thought he looked very pleased with their input. His tours were always booked up well in advance.

What will I do next? Suzanne thought to herself. She heard someone humming an old familiar cowboy ballad, "Back in the Saddle Again."

Someone was very happy with their ride. Benny Jo was really happy to see Suzanne again and came up to be petted and played with. She always demanded a little attention after an absence just to reassure herself she was not forgotten. The little dog came from a good home and a person who had loved her and given her a lot of attention, then died. It must have been a very lonely time for the little dog until Suzanne had found her needing a home.

Suzanne was very tired even though the horse had done all the walking. During the tour the group had been lectured to notice every interesting feature on the tour plus all the flora and fauna.

When she went back home to Ark City, she was going to know a lot about Oklahoma. Suzanne wondered if there were horse camps to attend in Kansas for tenderfeet who didn't know anything about ranching or horses.

She had decided to bring her diary up to date and list all the interesting facts she could remember each day. This would take a little bit of composing and thought while she rested up from the ride. She fell fast asleep with Benny Jo settled down beside her.

Most of the campers were resting or fixing their fishing rods for fishing. Everyone agreed they had enjoyed their morning horseback ride very much. Bill and Valerie who had camp watch that morning were scheduled for the horseback ride the next morning.

It was so much fun for everyone. They were looking forward to it very much!

Oh, the horseback ride had been a wonderful adventure for Suzanne. She had not been around the critters very much being a city kid. This was sure to be a great adventure. The horses were gentle and well-trained to reign commands.

Every day they walked the same trails carrying nervous novice horseback riders. The trail wound up the mountain carefully and the path might have seemed adventurous for some of the people but was "old hat" to all the horses.

Suzanne felt she had missed a lot of things by being a "city kid" only visiting farms occasionally. They would be fed a lot of information by their hosts of the care and grooming of their steeds during the day and each beautiful view was brought to the group's attention with a lot of information about the flora and fauna.

The thought of donuts and coffee upon the crest of their ride cheered her on. Everyone had brought cameras except Suzanne. This was the one time she would enjoy and remember without a pictorial scene snap. Maybe it was a mistake but she thought riding the horse would be all she could handle without dragging a heavy camera alongside.

Oh well, when they returned they were promised a good picture of each rider alone on his horse for a few extra dollars. The scenery was beautiful and at the top side each rider could rest a bit with their coffee and donuts before mounting for the ride back down.

Suzanne felt sorry for the little horse that carried the big fat man who complained all the time. The only way he could get back down the trail was "shut up and ride"…or walk!

Of course the leader was courteous, but the continual complaints must have been waring on his nerves. He had the complete sympathy of all the riders. The top of the mountain was a glorious experience when the sunrise came up over the top. The valley below was awesome, very little mist. Everyone was truly awed. Their guide gave a little nature talk just before they mounted to start the ride back down to camp. He had to help hoist the fat man back up on his horse.

Phil called Suzanne from Riverside to see how she was getting along. He and Frankie were really enjoying their time with grandkids seeing all the sites including Disney World, boating trip to Catalina and all kinds of good food and fun.

Suzanne assured him she was well taken care of with her new biker friends and had no more encounters with the bank robbers. On top of everything else, the park police were very vigilant and Warika camp patrol was very reassuring.

This report eased Phil's mind and he presumed the bank robbers had all the cash now in their their possession. Surely by now they would have been content to spend their ill-gotten gains and leave his sister alone.

Suzanne enjoyed telling him about her horseback ride through the trails at Warika. Maybe he would want to take his family to Warika for a camping trip sometime when they visited Kansas. There were a lot of other sites like Crystal Caverns up north near the Salt Plaines for vacations.

There was only one thing that bothered Phil in his talk with Suzanne. She had mentioned a mini biker who looked so funny as he passed their camp one or two times during her first two days at camp. Phil wondered why anyone would travel to camp on such a small uncomfortable vehicle. It seemed to have no room to carry camping supplies unless he was coupled up with another person in a bigger mode of travel and just used the mini bike for transport around camp. That said, Phil decided to ask the Duncan Police Captain to investigate the mini bike camper to find out his name.

Bill and Valerie had left early in the morning while Suzanne and Benny Jo were still snuggly asleep in their little cocoon wraps.

Suzanne wondered if she should get up and dress to be able to offer breakfast help.

Judy and Neal had signed up for breakfast duty that morning. Jim and Kate were doing clean up KP for later. It was easy with paper plates, cups and carefulness.

Suzanne decided it would be better to do KP clean up duty instead of cooking because the cooks were so proficient. They were used to doing their job and everything was planned so well for the meal. She didn't mind volunteering for clean-up crew like scrubbing and disinfecting the tables for meals.

The bikers let her contribute to the meal expenses just so she wouldn't feel left out when they shopped for food. Several of their party wanted to rent canoes and paddle around fishing. Suzanne was not an avid fisherman woman, so she elected to do something different. Maybe look over the museum displays. There were plenty of extraordinary things to discover amidst all the displays.

Benny Jo did not know what Suzanne had on her mind, but decided she had better tag along for guard dog duty in case of trouble. The wild raccoons were driving her crazy with the marauding antics at night after the camp quieted down. She would have liked to grab one and shake it to death, but was never able to catch one.

Bart finished his shower and shave and felt much better because of the good breakfast of pancake, sausage, and java Tobi had provided. He decided to come clean and tell Tobi why he was at Warika Park casing the bikers camp. It was going to be demeaning and tough to face up to his mistake with the bank bag, but he reasoned Tobi would probably understand better than Patty would have.

Tobi would accept the situation and try to help reason out a plan where Patty would have gone ballistic with accusations, and been no help whatsoever. Bart might as well take his medicine and fess up. When Bart approached Tobi's campsite he sat down and stared off into the woods. Tobi sat quietly waiting while Bart stirred up his thoughts.

"I hid the bank bag in the Kansas woman's wheel well with most of the money in it. She ran off in the car but, I'm sure she doesn't know the money bag is still there," Bart shook his head. "What a dolt I am!"

Silence from Tobi, just quiet breathing. Then, he sighed to himself. He understood the feeling of dissatisfaction that Bart must have felt. It was the frustration of seeing that money bag roll away out of his grasp and the thought that he did it all by his own carelessness. He could not put the blame on anyone else.

Well, Tobi was smart enough to know Bart needed a strong shoulder to lean on and not have someone like Patty to tell him how dumb his action was!

This was the time to buddy-up and help but not blame Bart. The reality of the situation was hopelessly apparent. Hearing the confession in cold blood was bad enough. Tobi was just glad no one had gotten hurt over the whole fiasco.

Tobi realized it would be smart not to damage what little bravado Bart had left in him. Patty would have been tempted to brow beat him into another fit of anger.

Men always hung together. The fact that Bart had not fired the gun at the fleeing car was a good thing. That would have been really bad.

Tobi let out another sigh, "Well, we need to plan on a way to get a look in that car while it's unattended."

"That's the problem," Bart snorted. "They never leave camp without one couple standing guard over their motorcycles." Bart laughed. "They think that is what they are guarding."

"The dog that sleeps in the car with the woman, I can handle with sleeping pills but, I don't know how to drug the woman."

"It's possible she might take off for Kansas anytime too," said Tobi. "I don't think she plans to be with the bikers for their whole trip."

"I have wracked my brain and only come up with a way to put the dog to sleep with pills," Bart sighed.

"Two heads are better than one," Tobi said. "We will plan a way to get in that van or else! Maybe it would be better to let the woman drive back to Kansas where she would be alone in her car. I could handle something like that. It's the motorcycle escort that has me stymied! They guard their vehicles like they were the crown prince jewels. They really don't know about the money yet. Unless some wise cracker thinks up the scenario!"

Bart was really disgusted with himself and everyone else in his way to fame and fortune.

"What have you got in mind, Tobi?" he asked. "It's now more dangerous with all those people around all the time and I don't know how long we got before she goes home to Kansas."

Bart replied, "Maybe it would be best to get in that car after she leaves by herself to go home."

"Do you suppose no one will disturb her car?" Tobi asked. "What if some smart cop thinks to search it thoroughly?" Tobi was thinking out loud as he paced back and forth. "It's just a chance we would have to take."

Bart jumped up. "No, no, no, I don't want to wait and drive myself crazy, I'm already half way insane now."

"Okay, okay, we will form a plan." Tobi said.

Suzanne and Mary Jo went to the women's shower to get their hair washed. The morning was cool enough to be pleasant but not too cold for a morning shower. Suzanne had both bath soap and detergent to wash her laundry and they stayed in the showers a long time to get everything clean.

Doing KP kitchen clean up and garbage detail had made Suzanne use up all the energy she had, plus extra.

"I'm really gonna conk out tonight," she told Mary Jo.

Suzanne planned a restful day and a long walk to visit the grocery, museum store, and sight see the hatchery and grounds. Maybe buy a few souvenirs to take home. She picked up a water bottle to take along on her walk.

Suzanne liked to find interesting rocks for her collection at home if there were any pretty stones lying around. Benny Jo tagged along with her not really caring where they went. She just loved to chase the raccoons. They must have walked a mile down to the entrance gate to the park.

The breeze was just cool enough to keep them comfortable. Suzanne let Benny Jo run free mostly and didn't make her use the leash unless traffic came their way.

Suzanne and her dog, Benny Jo, started to hike slowly around the beautiful lake. They didn't plan to walk far, stopping to investigate every little cover and quirk of flora and farina they found different along the shore line. It was peaceful and soothing to look out over the water.

Suzanne put the leash on Benny Jo when they came to a bunch of ducks swimming close to shore. Dachshunds were born and bred to kill birds instinctively. It wasn't Benny Jo's fault that she would quickly grab a duck and wring its neck just for fun. This was bred in her and impossible to train out. With the leash on, she knew she would not be allowed to grab and kill any of the ducks.

Ducks were off the ticket for lunch today, *her* lunch anyway. Fried chicken seemed to be enjoyed often by people and a few bites were offered her on occasion, but swimming fowls were off limits to Benny Jo's dismay.

They passed the spot where Tobi was camping and Bart was having a meal with his friend. Bart noticed their approach before Tobi, and turned his back to the road as they passed by. Bart was still mad at the woman and it was hard to hold his rage in as she passed on their road. His silent vow was strengthened by his rage. He didn't want to wait longer to search that van, period!! Tonight was the night for his revenge!

Dope the dog, hit the woman over the head to knock her out, grab his money, then run. Bart was still shaking with rage long after Suzanne and her dog had walked past their campsite. His thinking was clearly unstable and it took a long time before his temper cooled down.

Tobi was wise to keep silent. He knew exactly what was going through Bart's mind and how much control was needed to remain calm. Tobi hoped Bart could continue to control himself for fear of the many times he had lost it in the past. Usually it was Patty that provoked Bart's rage.

Bart had slapped Patty around a few times when he couldn't control his rage at her useless nagging. Tobi was glad Patty was not with them, left safely back in her hometown. If he was going to be able to help Bart control his rage, he didn't need Patty along yapping at them both.

Tobi carefully packed all the breakfast provisions back in his big ice chest. He watched Bart slowly cool back down after the woman and her dog passed by. She looked small, but athletic, and might be a problem if they could not get her away from the car with her dog.

Tobi wondered if there was any way possible to drug both the woman and her dog. He did not ask Bart, however, because Bart was not in a good mood yet and might jump up and do something wrong without thinking first.

"You need a little cool-down time now Bart," he said in a soothing voice. "Maybe fish a little and contemplate a good idea. Maybe something we haven't thought of yet."

He turned away to fix his ever present fishing rod with bait. Tobi thought fishing was a good way to relax and plan. It seemed to calm Bart down from the tenseness of seeing the woman and her dog again.

"Yea, that sounds good to me," Bart agreed and sighed again. "We can work our way along the water and scout all we want to with a fishing rod," Bart spoke up. "It will be good cover too."

So their mood changed to hopeful relaxation and planning their next move under the cover of fishing. Tobi fixed both of his fishing rods so they could fish together. It would be a good way to relax and plan together while watching all the campsites as they walked the river.

An innocent looking fisherman would never be suspect as long as he really fished, caught and kept. Tobi liked to eat fish and really knew how to prepare them over a campfire too. Their cover was perfect and as the sun got hotter overhead, Tobi had caught enough fish to have a good fish fry supper.

Suzanne and Benny Jo walked and walked and enjoyed every little flower and rock formation that looked different. Suzanne was always in the habit of picking up pretty rocks, different flowers or odd things in an outdoor walk. She was a true nature lover and the little dachshund dog loved to walk and just sniff out all the different colors she came across.

They walked together and many times one of the wives would be with them exploring the museums and stores. This place was a healing ground that calmed Suzanne's nerves down from the frightful kidnapping experience she had been through.

Suzanne thought to herself the trip with the Harley bunch was the best medicine that could have been provided to erase the horrible experience of the bank robbery in Kingfisher!

She sometimes wondered what the two felons had done when they discovered she had outwitted them and escaped from the park rest stop. How had they managed to get back to their own places?

She stopped to think what she would have done if they had just dumped her out on the highway. She could not go to a police station and complain. She didn't even know their names and hadn't seen their faces.

The only identifying mark she remembered was an ugly scorpion tattoo on the man's left arm. She did remember telling the Duncan Police Captain of the identifying mark. It did seem vague at the time, but she found herself always looking for the scorpion mark on everyone she passed by.

Suzanne didn't know this, but the Duncan Police Captain was investigating every tattoo parlor owner with this little bit of information to get a name of anyone with a scorpion tattoo. He had many towns to work through and it would take some time, but he was confident he would find the man with the scorpion tattoo because it was a unique, distinct mark. Not very many people chose to have a permanent tattoo on their torso and not everyone was fond of a scorpion one at that. Only someone with a strange, quirky personality.

One day the Harley gang decided to swim in the resort pool. Some of the guys fancied themselves to be good at diving and had excelled at the sport while in high school. It was a great way to relax, stay cool and acquire some tan. Suzanne offered to guard camp for them if they all wanted to swim.

She thought it was her duty to join in all their chores and do her part. They all vetoed that idea, however, because she was their guest of honor. Going beyond the call of duty, she did a lot of the kitchen clean-up chores and went out of her way to help in all the odd jobs around their camp.

Julia and Art volunteered to be camp sitters while everyone else swam or shopped. Art was not particularly fond of swimming and he figured the guys would welcome his suggestion. Also, he wouldn't have K.P. duty if he was camp guard for the day.

Art planned to do a lot of relaxing in the afternoon shade. After two days of hiking and horseback riding, tennis and fishing, he was ready for a restful afternoon of camp guarding. Julia always puttered around painting pictures or taking snapshots of the interesting scenery. She also needed a time out for contemplation.

Everyone agreed to let them have their day of camp guard. Swimming of a morning was cool too, because the heat of the afternoon sun had not yet arrived. They could swim and not worry about sunburn until after lunch and, if they were tired, they could work in a little siesta.

Swimming in the pool was so relaxing and Suzanne really enjoyed herself. Benny Jo, of course, was not allowed in the fenced-in pool area. She stood outside the fence looking sadly at all the folks having fun. It didn't seem fair to be excluded from all their gayety, but the dog had to accept the fact she was not allowed in the swimming pool. She was allowed to wade around in the lake. To her doggy way of thinking, it just didn't make sense. People were odd at times.

Chapter 9

Tobi came over to the pool and watched the crowd swimming. He studied each one to familiarize himself with their faces. He concluded they were all very agile and well-muscled, not a crowd that he would want to tangle with. Tobi wondered if it would be better to hold off until the woman went alone to her Kansas home.

He knew her name after they had researched the newspaper stories about the motorcycle group. Tobi was the cautious type of thinker. He knew the police captain would soon decide to search the car more thoroughly, if he had any brains at all. The bad part was he could not show any curiosity by questioning the police about their case because that would automatically involve him.

Tobi was safe from prosecution if he remained incognito and let Bart do all the dangerous parts. If Tobi was connected to Bart in any covert action he would be suspected of the bank crime; and that, he did not want.

Oh, the irony of it all was, Tobi wanted some of the money too. He was not particularly fond of Bart's tempestuous nature and he pitied the poor guy for his stupidity. When Bart and Patty had come up to him and told him of their plans to rob the bank in Kingfisher, he was amused and didn't really take them seriously at first.

He thought they were a couple of crazy kids off on a lark surely wound up on drugs. Then Bart presented the easy job of driving the get-away car to him to share one-third of the loot.

Easy money, Tobi thought, *with Bart doing the dangerous part.*

Well he had not taken Bart's impulsiveness into the equation - that's why it sounded so fool-proof. Now he was more involved by his own curiosity or compassion and a little bit of greedy covetousness. He wanted some of the money.

Bart noticed the dog had trotted off to the swimming pool so he decided to sneak over to the cycle camp and case the van site again while everyone had gone to the pool. Art seemed to be snoozing, but he was not asleep. Julia was nosing around taking pictures of everything.

Not good, Bart decided. *Not cool at all!*

Bart stayed hidden back in the trees and used his binoculars to observe the bikers camp activity. Each day there was a different couple to guard but they were always alert and never caught asleep or absent. It almost seemed impossible to infiltrate their camp. He wondered what they would do it he kidnapped their dog and held her for ransom.

The dog was the only one vulnerable and unable to identify me, he thought.

But the ransom might not be given for a dog's rescue. Bart wondered how much Suzanne loved the little mutt. Would she give up the money to him if he told her where to find it or would she be hard-hearted enough to part with her pet? She was an unknown quantity, after all.

Bart was getting desperate to try anything! He decided to talk this idea over with Tobi first, and not go off half-cocked on his own, like the bank heist. That was the one flaw in his bank job idea. He had not stuck strictly with the plan and everything had gone downhill - kaput!

Two heads were always better at planning. Bart decided to find Tobi quickly and put the idea out for approval. Good old Tobi was a wise old owl. While Bart thought up all the good plans, Tobi knew how to appraise the outcome.

The group in the swimming pool slowly sunned themselves and soon got hungry for lunch. What had they planned for lunch?

Baked ham was in the big crock kettle with yams slowly heating up. Also, green beans with dill butter and sliced onions to season them properly in a big pan.

The swimmers appetites grew larger and larger until about 12:00 and they could not put off eating any longer. Everyone was famished, well exercised, warmed or cooked and ready to dry off and eat. Benny Jo was happy, happy, happy, and racing around the group as they emerged from the fence-enclosed pool.

Everyone was really satisfied with lunch and swimming had given them all good appetites. The ham and sweet potatoes were well lathered with butter and the green beans were very well seasoned. Everyone stuffed themselves and decided to walk and exercise a bit before going back to swim in the late afternoon and evening.

Suzanne tried to take an afternoon nap, then day mares ruined any rest she might have achieved as she relived the awful kidnapping event over again.

This time she was shot and thrown over the Canadian bridge in pain and had to swim for her life when two big fish tried to swallow her on the way down to the bottom of the river. One of the fish wore a silly hat on its face and the other wore a stocking cap and looked more like a scorpion than a fish. What a horrible nightmare, Suzanne decided, even if it was in the daytime.

She felt her face to see if she had a sunburn but her skin felt cool under the trees which shaded the campsite. Valerie asked Suzanne if she was up to traveling to another state park. One the bikers had been to before but one she had not seen yet. Suzanne thought Valerie was very kind to invite her along for another day or two of their travels. After all, she was just an uninvited nuisance to their travels and one that needed constant protection.

Suzanne had learned many new things from the group and it was always just in time to keep her from harms way. It seemed she had lots to learn about bike and travel etiquette. Suzanne decided she would poll the opinions of each separate couple before she would make that decision. If the whole group was not of one accord, she did not want to be a point of dissension in their group decision. She had only agreed to accompany them to their first location as an invited guest.

A lot of the campers were intrigued by the motorcycle group and wanted to visit with them and the group felt more confident and at ease with strangers.

They decided their group was perfectly safe now and all the people in the park were bon-a-fide vacation campers. They let down their safeguard a little more but not entirely. No one seemed dangerous and all the vacationers had lots to entertain them.

Suzanne weighed the pros and cons of traveling more days with the cycle group. They were so hospitable and fun to be with, but she did feel like a "5th" wheel. She was the only single traveler with the group and the only partner she had was Benny Jo, her dog. True, she was never made to feel like an outsider.

In fact, this bunch made her feel very welcome, because they were all so friendly. She talked it over that night with her brother, Phil and wife, Frankie. It was very good to have them for a sounding board and they always gave good advice.

First question Frankie asked was, "Do you feel safe traveling with the group?"

"Of course, of course and I admit to being a little uneasy on the road alone," she replied. "Of course, being with a group seemed very secure against a long road trip home alone."

It was possible to get almost all the way home if she stayed with the group but she didn't want to wear out her welcome or continue to be a burden.

Suzanne had to admit she still had nightmares where she was killed by the kidnappers and she knew it would take a while before she could quit looking over her shoulder for more trouble.

"Why?" Frankie asked.

It was impossible to explain her nightmares because Suzanne didn't understand them either. Nothing in her fearful dreams had actually happened to her. Most of them were not understandable.

Phil and Frankie decided Suzanne needed to hear more about their fun times instead of being grilled about her unhappy event. So they relayed all the family news and ended their talk with information about the fun times had with their children.

After they spoke, Phil called the Duncan Police Captain to see if there were any new developments in the case. He really did not expect to be informed of any new lead they might have but only hoped to hear good news so he could quit worrying. Safety for his sister was what he needed to hear.

Of course the police captain could not reveal anything critical to his case. However, he knew the police captain would not try to sugar coat the case. Nothing good had developed yet, but two people were being investigated.

The Duncan Police Captain decided Phil deserved to be informed of all the progress he had made in the bank heist case that was not strategic to the capture. Besides, Phil was a good sounding board to bounce ideas off about this particular case.

Phil was only concerned about his sister's safety, but he was a clever thinker and gave the police captain any thoughts that came into his mind.

A very clever mind, the police captain thought. *Phil would have made a good police detective.*

One point Phil asked him about was why the bank robbers would not have a sure driver for their get-a-way car instead of grabbing just anyone who happened to come along. This point was noted in the police captain's notebook of ideological thinking. There had to be a better get-a-way plan than just grabbing anyone. What had happened to the get-a-way car and driver who was surely left behind? It was a very disturbing thought! You never plan a bank robbery without a good get-a-way ending plan. Something had delayed their driver! Another unidentified person to deal with and one who would never reveal his identity.

The only thing that might tie the third person to the crime would be the allure of his share in the money. This was one reason the police captain held off searching the car again. He was never sure that a reporter following him would keep quiet about his actions of searching the van.

It would be hard to muzzle the press. Every day one reporter visited the police for news to print about any action the police did on any case. While he was thankful for all the good press reports of police action, this was one case he did not want to give information on yet. He had to keep quiet or his trap might never be sprung to catch the thieves.

He decided to call the motorcycle's group cop and tell him about a possible third felon, the driver, and why it might include two men along with the woman. The unidentified driver and get-away car that was too late to pick the robbers up.

The Duncan Police Captain called the motorcycle cop to check and see if he had seen any suspicious characters or if he had any new information about the group activities. What was the woman planning to do now? Was she planning to travel on home alone to Kansas?

If she decided to leave the motorcycle group the police captain planned to follow her home to Kansas and would inform her of this fact. It might make her feel safer but he did not want to cut any of the vacation plans short so he kept this fact to himself. The police captain was running a background check on several of the campers in the Warika Park.

Two lone fishermen were also included in his survey. No one looked suspicious, but the police captain knew felons always could portray innocence and look average to blend in with their background. What could be more evasive than to pack a fishing rod?

Actually most of the people who fished cooked and ate their catch. No one acted strange. One of the two fishermen slept a lot in the afternoon but that could be due to relations and vacationing without working worries.

He could not connect a place of employment to both of the fishermen and this was his only puzzle. Surely they had a job that enabled them to take an extended vacation.

Another thing was in the police captain's mind. The woman who helped rob the bank - where would she be? Would the woman stay with her partner or would she stay separate? Would they always hang together? What was the story of this relationship? Since they did very little talking in their getaway car ride very little information was noted. It was almost like playing a part for them, an exciting adventure gone awry. The captain did not know if he should be looking for three people together or not. Would the man just dump the woman and go on alone or did he really need her at all?

The police captain decided someone should look for the scorpion tattoo mark on the left wrist of each man at the Warika Park but how could this be accomplished? Privacy and individual rights were rigidly followed by all law officers. There was no way he could force everyone at the park to bare their left arms and suffer through a police survey.

The police captain would need to be very careful of individual privacy laws because, after all, Oklahoma is not a police state. Each person was allowed perfect, peaceful freedom in Oklahoma, even bank robbers until they acted up or created a bad situation with another person.

He did ask the Harley cycle police troopers to snoop around for the scorpion tattoo mark on a man's left wrist without seeming to be overly interested. This fact was all it took for the troopers to be on a clue alert.

However, he was told not to make this fact public news yet. The woman already knew about the scorpion tattoo so no one else would have been alarmed with this extra fact. In fact, maybe Suzanne had already told them everything she could recall about the bank felons.

The trooper didn't know about the tattoo until it was mentioned to him, which seemed to indicate Suzanne did not clue all the Harley people into every detail. The police captain did want the Harley cycle trooper to know all the facts and that was one reason he checked in with Danny frequently for updates and any new occurrences the travelers might encounter.

The police captain needed all the clues he could garner even if they were inconsequential. Danny knew what to look for mostly for danger.

It seemed the morning had been calm enough by everyone swimming in the pool together. Very few extra campers joined in the morning swim. There had been a lot of extra folks on the horseback trail the day before but, no one had been overly nosy or friendly with Suzanne.

They only had one grouch on the trail ride, an older, fat fellow who did not fit the bank robber's description at all because he was noisy and obnoxious.

Suzanne remembered the Osage Indian Tribe had settled up north near her hometown of Ark City and the Otoe Missouria Tribe had settled south of Ponca City near the waters. Even then the tribes were pretty close to one another and could have been blood brothers.

Many artifacts were discovered on farms in the area when farmers planted their wheat and cotton near her home town of Ark City. The Indians from Chilocco School liked to participate in the town's celebration at Halloween times of the big Arkalalah parade October 31 each year.

Everyone came to watch the colorful floats and carnivals that. School bands from small Kansas towns participated, and Oklahoma neighboring towns were highlighted and judged for prizes. She didn't know so many Indian tribes were located in Oklahoma until this trip, which was very informative giving tribal headquarters information.

The fact that Arkansas City is located between two rivers made it a prime location for Indian tribes to reside before the white settlers came. An old Indian tradition that circulated said there would never be a tornado come down to land between the two Arkansas and Walnut rivers. One might pass over head, but could not cross on land where the two rivers met.

Suzanne liked this tradition because she felt the two rivers protected her home from harm.

Home, she thought to herself, *so warm and safe and comfortable.*

Never again would she forget how comforting and safe a good home could be. We really do not appreciate what God has given to us until we lose it all and feel helpless.

When Suzanne thought about all the fun she was having with her motorcycle family friends, she really didn't want to go on home alone. Her brother, Phil, had mentioned the van had several hiding places for anyone to put a bag of money.

This thought made her wonder if she could make a search alone even though it might take a lot of muscle power she didn't have or extra tools to look into the car body. She finally decided after much thought that she really needed the expertise of a strong muscular mechanic to search the van.

Maybe the Duncan Police Captain should be in charge if he thought the Kingfisher bank money might still be in her car. However, she did not want to appear to be a bossy female telling a police captain what he should do, so she decided to wait and see if he thought about searching further for the bank's money.

Suzanne was sure he would have all the tools at his disposal and the know-how to do the search right. She relaxed again and decided to just enjoy her unexpected vacation with her new friends as long as they would tolerate her presence.

Chapter 10

A barn dance was mentioned the night before as the group ate supper over their campfire. A neighboring church was sponsoring a get together featuring a real fun night of family barn dancing. Mary Jo explained to Suzanne how it worked. Each family formed a line with children and parents in a circular fashion and danced together.

Of course, you had to follow the instructions hollered out by the emcee and you had to know the steps involved too. This might be something she would have to watch for a while before she learned what to do. It might take a lot of practice, but it was all good fun and families could learn to do it together. It was a good thing moms and dads could take their youngsters along with them and families could enjoy together.

Plenty of exercise was involved and an invitation was issued to folks at the park to join in. Food would be available but, everyone decided to donate to help out with the cost. These folks were very good to help out and support one another. The good pioneer spirit still lived in these Oklahoma friends she had found and she didn't want to let them go, ever.

The barn dance was something Suzanne had never experienced before. The seating on the side line was your own folding chairs or sit on a bale of hay. The church sponsoring the event provided the music and food and welcomed everyone at the door.

The barn was big and had plenty of space in the center for all the families to dance. A lot of teenagers accompanied their folks for the fun and seemed to know the steps called out by the emcee.

Suzanne was awed and felt kind of dumb because she really had forgotten all the dance steps called out by the emcee except for one: the Do-se-do.

She decided to sit down and watch a while. Katy sat down beside her and was explaining some of the steps as the group danced around the room to the music. Each time the emcee hollered out a step everyone in the room seemed to know what to do.

Of course, there were a few just learning but with their arms all entwined, a mistake was soon corrected. All the little folks had to do was watch mom and dad and copy their footsteps.

The motorcycle group already knew all the steps called out so this was not a puzzle to them. Growing up in Oklahoma seemed to include knowing all the barn dance steps. Line dancing was a lot of fun and exercise.

Suzanne picked up the print outs at the door describing dance steps for each dance the caller would call during the evening. They had interesting names and looked inviting to try out. Suzanne wondered if she would have the grace to enter in the lines dancing. At first everything looked difficult, so she sat down to read the moves for the first "line dance" called out as the families lined up. "County Line" was called out and mostly everybody knew what to do.

Suzanne studied the dance instructions as she watched them played out before her. It was astounding! The whole group moved to do the steps in perfect moves together!

County Line Dance Instructions:
20 count - 4 wall line dance
Music - any cha-cha music
1-2-3-4
Rock back on right foot turning body slightly to the right
Rock forward on left foot
Cha-cha in place
1-2-3-4
Rock back on left foot turning bod slightly to the left
Rock forward on right foot

Cha-cha in place
1-2-3-4
Rock back on right foot turning body slightly to the right
Rock forward on left foot
Cha-cha in place
1-2-3-4
Step forward on left foot
Slide right foot behind left foot
Step forward on left foot
Slide right foot behind left foot
1-2-3-4
Cross left foot over right foot
Step back on right foot
Cha-cha in place
Begin dance again, but when you rock forward on left foot make a 1/4
turn to the left...counter-clockwise.

Stray Cat Strut
32 count....4 well line dance
Music (any upbeat 4/4 count song)
1-2-3-4-5-6-7-8
Touch right heel in front
Step right foot beside left foot
Touch left heel in front
Step left foot beside right foot
Touch right heel in front
Step right foot beside left foot
Touch left heel in front
Step left foot beside right foot
1-2-3-4-5-6-7-8
Tap right heel in front two times
Tap right toe behind two times

Touch right heel in front
Touch right toe behind
Touch right heel in front
Touch right heel behind
1-2-3-4-5-6-7-8
Strut forward 4 times...set heel in front and then drop entire foot to
floor...right, left, right, left
1-2-3-4-5-6-7-8
Cross right foot over left foot
Step back on left foot
Step right foot to the side while making a 1/4 turn to the right
Step left foot beside right foot
Cross right foot over left foot
Step back on left foot
Step to the side with right foot
Step left foot beside right foot

Suzanne studied those dance step instructions and watched the dancers diligently. She did want to join in, but wanted to do the steps perfectly before a crowd.

Some people had natural grace, but not all, she thought as she watched.

It did help to be part of a line of dancers who really knew what they were doing. By the end of the evening, she had finally got up the nerve to enter a couple of different dances and really enjoyed the movements. She had also consumed two Dr. Peppers and a dozen cookies provided by the host.

Suzanne began to wonder if there were a lot of barn dances in Kansas and had she missed out on them. She decided to investigate once she got back home again. Benny Jo, her little dog had climbed out of the car so she went outside to put her back in again.

Barn dances took a lot of energy if you danced every dance, she decided. It would be okay to sit and rest occasionally. Phil, her brother, called again to hear what the group was doing. He laughed when she told him about learning the barn dance steps.

He was relieved when she told him the home front was quiet and peaceful. Phil still reminded her to check every arm for the tattoo of the scorpion. He really had confidence in the cycle policeman that led the group, but he was afraid Suzanne might be letting down her guard.

It sounded like she was having a lot of fun! Barn dancing, he and Frankie would have to investigate when they returned. It might be good for a group to exercise for health together as they learned the steps in family style.

This was a new way to exercise he had never experienced! Barn dancing was a past time old settlers had enjoyed years ago. The new age had completely ignored the old ways by adding their own new fads of weird movement.

The Duncan Police Captain had reassured Phil the park was still peaceful and he had two people he was investigating with a background of checks regarding work habits and environment. There was nothing important to be concerned about.

Phil had a lot of good news to tell Suzanne about their vacation. They had enjoyed parasailing behind a boat one day. Both enjoyed it tremendously and planned to repeat their experience.

Frankie's brother had been a helicopter pilot in the army and Phil wanted to take flying instructions when they returned home. He wondered if it would be hard to find a school that offered helicopter training nearby. Maybe in Wichita?

He planned to investigate everything when they returned home. Both Frankie and Suzanne wanted to be included in the flying lessons. Expense was what they needed to calculate, of course. If it was too expensive for all three, they would defer to Phil to experience this alone.

Nothing ventured, nothing gained, they thought.

Suzanne patted Benny Jo and scratched her ears which she always wanted. The little dog loved as much attention as she could get.

More than she needed, Suzanne thought!

A pampered pup that always craves affection. The more the better! The parking lot at the barn was well-lit and well-supervised for the barn dance party so Suzanne and Benny Jo felt well protected sitting nearest to the barn doors.

All-in-all, the evening had been a great experience and lots of fun. By the time the evening wore down, everyone was tired and well-exercised.

They thought they should take up a good collection to help out for all the refreshments and band music the church had provided. Everyone wanted to donate, so a big Stetson hat was passed around then placed in the host's hands at the door. Suzanne decided it was well worth her $20 donation.

Back at the campfire, Suzanne brushed Benny Jo's fur coat and inspected her for any unwanted ticks before bedtime. This was a nightly ritual for protection while camping outdoors. Benny Jo thought humans were very weird in all their ritual dancing and parading in circles around inside the barn. She didn't even like the band's music because it hurt her ears and was squeaky too!

Benny Jo had watched most of the evening dance ritual from the barn door. There were so many people parading around in the barn she was afraid of being stepped on by some big sharp heeled boots. There were so many people promenading around it was dangerous to a little dachshund. Just like a big herd of animals stomping the grounds.

She was glad when it was time to turn out the lights and go home. Suzanne tucked Benny Jo in her little bed cocoon and slowly followed the biker family back to the park. It was getting close to eleven o'clock when they all pulled in to their parking places. The dog was snoring, which sounded funny to Suzanne. She didn't know dogs did that in their sleep.

She slowly backed her car into place and kept very quiet so as to not disturb any other campers that might be asleep. They left one dim lamp aglow as they settled into sleeping bags and fixed windows screens in place.

Only one person sat quietly watching the group settle down for the night. He was hidden among the underbrush of fir trees up against a slight hill overlooking the camp. He wondered if they were all so tired a fast visit would not disturb them. The fast visit had a drawback however, because the woman and the dog were so near to the bank bag, it would be impossible without drugging both into a deep sleep.

Quiet settled down over the camp as everyone climbed into their sleeping bag. The moon was at full quarter and shown down brightly on their camp. It was one light that couldn't be put out unless a cloud covered it.

The man on the hill decided a rainy night would be the best time to pilfer a car; even then, it would be dangerous. So far the weather had been perfect for all the campers at Warika, mild and clear. Weather was always risky.

Drugging a dog and predicting rainy weather at the same time seemed very difficult to the man on the hill. His mind raced with all the alternatives.

At the barn dance, the outdoor lighting and activity pretty much assured them a safe night. Even though the dancing kept most folks inside the barn, there were a lot of others roaming in and out. Also, the dog had bedded down inside the van and it was parked right next to the open barn door.

If they would just let up on their guard duty routine one day, his problems would be solved. But they never wavered from routine.

Just like a bunch of fuddy-duddy teachers, never falter from your guard duty detail. Bart was slowly running out of cash and it jolted him to find out from Tobi that Patty had withheld a big wad of cash in her purse and let him hand over another thousand to keep her quiet.

It just went to prove you never could trust a dame. This thought made him double mad at the woman and her dog! Women, in general, were bad trouble and he should always keep that in mind.

Night settled in quietly and everyone was sound asleep resting. Bart decided to creep over and see if he could peer into the van window without causing a ruckus. He needed to move a little to rest his cramped bones from an awkward position.

Maybe they were all so tired he could get a little closer. He stopped short! What was he thinking? He would only have one chance at the wheel well and it shouldn't be when everyone was there! He needed to wait until only a couple guarded the camp.

Wake up, Bart told himself. No mistakes could be made at his one last attempt to retrieve the cash. What would the group decide to do tomorrow? Maybe he could risk joining in if it was swimming.

Don't be too obvious, was his motto. Morning came quickly after all the exercise the group had the previous evening. Tired bones slowly roused and began their daily exercise - breakfast and bathroom duties at the shower house.

Julia and Art, Neal and Judy were fixing breakfast. It smelled delicious in the morning air. The group had been blessed with perfect weather without any accidents. They enjoyed good health thanks to their perfectly planned meals with plenty of veggies and fruit. Thanks went to Lila and Kate for planning the daily menus and purchasing fresh produce for each day.

Their expertise in planning menus and using different herbs to bring out flavors was nothing short of a miracle. Those gals were superb cooks over an open campfire stewpot. No one complained of upset stomach or any other ailment all week long. Everything went along smoothly. The vacation was the first time the group had been invited to a barn dance by the local Baptist church. Jim thought the barn dance had been a perfect addition to their cycle trip. He hoped the dance would occur each vacation and be an added attraction for everyone.

Breakfast smelled great: mushroom omelets with avocado butter, waffles with honey and orange juice, grape juice and coffee, of course. No breakfast was complete without coffee. It gave one an added dose of energy to start the day. Food was always important to Jim, who thought maybe it was his time to start a diet with extra exercise to work off a few unwanted pounds.

What would the group want to do today? Maybe another day to fish or swim? A nature hike? At just that moment he caught a movement up on top of the hill behind their campsite. Was that a figure with binoculars spying on their camp? He thought he should quietly bring this to Danny's attention - the state trooper who watched over the group with an eagle eye.

Quietly Jim went to Dan's sleeping tent and whispered his information. Dan crept out rubbing his eyes but he had his binoculars with him. It was still early and morning light was not full yet. Their movements were cautious and slowly coordinated so as to not disturb the other sleepers. It was really too early for the whole group to be up and stirring around.

Danny decided to creep slowly out of view into the fir trees at camp side and see if he could recognize the peeper on the hill without stirring up a bunch of folks.

He didn't know if the person on the hill slope had night time goggles. If he did, he would soon move and might be traced back to his camp. Danny was dismayed that their camp might be under surveillance. It might mean more troubles were coming their way just as they were all relaxing and really enjoying themselves. Danny hated to put them all on edge. It just didn't seem fair to interrupt their serene complacency again.

He debated whether he should put them on alert again since Suzanne and her little dog were so much more relaxed. Danny really hated to scare them. He debated in his mind, *how should I handle the spying problem? How can I assure Suzanne I was handling their safety in the best possible way?*

Well, Dan decided he needed the expertise of the Duncan Police Captain, because he was sure he was providing all information to the Kingfisher Police, as well as Warika Park Control officials. The names given would not be correct.

Dan expected the ones spying on their camp to have aliases, even if he inspected enrollments given for spaces in Warika Park. Before alerting anyone else, he was going to find out who their spy was, then talk to the Duncan Police Captain.

In black garb, Dan quietly crawled to the outside of their camp. Slowly, he continued around about movement toward the stranger on the hill. All was quiet in the camp as Jim sat quietly watching the slow movements of Dan. He never moved or acted suspiciously in any way to alert the guy on the hilltop of their actions. Jim was just waiting for any sound from the hilltop to act and help Dan.

The quiet seemed so eerie that early in the morning. All that could be heard were nature sounds of running waters and soft bird coos. It was so quietly soothing, even the raccoons were asleep after their night of foraging for food. It was a shame their people were being spied upon by a little punk crook.

If he would just come out in the open they could grab him for good. Sneaking around in the dark put Jim's teeth on edge, as he had never dealt with a criminal before! The stranger on the hill quietly disappeared in the darkness before Dan could work his way around back and up the hill to intercept him.

At least they gave it a try commando style. Next time we'll set a trap for our spy. A good one, Dan decided with the help of Kingfisher Police.

The cycle group heard of another square dance close by the camp at another little nearby barn. It was hosted by one of the closest Baptist churches in a nearby small Oklahoma town. It was sure to be fun and the group decided to attend. It was a most relaxing kind of exercise and good for the whole family to participate.

The farmer's barn was near Hastings, Oklahoma, just far enough out in the country to be accessible to Warika campers. Everyone was looking forward to having a good time.

Suzanne got out her dance instructions and reviewed all the steps again. They seemed so relaxing and easy she thought she would have no trouble remembering them. She had bought a cowboy hat in the local gift shop, plus an Oklahoma t-shirt that pictured a horse with silver threads on it. The silver threads hung way down and swayed when you walked or danced in it.

Dan quickly contacted the Kingfisher police department with news of their night time stalker. The police captain was most interested in catching the desperado and promised to come up with a good plan on the night of the square dance.

Dan explained everything that had happened the night of surveillance and the police captain told him not to worry - he would have a squad of his own men surround the car while the group was in the barn.

He asked Dan to be sure the car was parked a few rows back from the barn door and sort of in the middle of a row of cars. Their plan put the cycles parked on the far side of the barn away from all the cars.

What to do with Benny Jo the dog? Dan knew Suzanne could not leave the dog penned up alone in the park, but Dan did not want Benny Jo to be left in the car alone in case the bank robber was at their dance.

If he could make sure the dog was in the barn, it would be okay, but the problem was to figure out how to confine the dog. The Kingfisher police captain counted on Dan to have Benny Jo at the dance.

Everything was going according to plan except where and how to keep Benny Jo safe and out of any action that might occur. Everywhere Suzanne went Benny Jo went along! Dan did not want to alert any of the group, except for Jim, of the Kingfisher police captain's plan. He discussed these plans with Jim and both racked their brains with different solutions. No harm must come to the little dog.

Plan one: Suzanne was not in on the police surveillance of her van. The dog must stay in the barn or, at best, out of the van at all times. Who could oversee the bathroom duty for Benny Jo? It seemed like this had to be Dan, so his wife would be barn dancing without him all evening but, Jim wanted to help dog sit. The dog must go to the barn dance because it was a given she was never left alone. Any plan to exclude the dog was not an option.

Benny Jo was well-trained and never let Suzanne out her sight if she was moving around. It Suzanne sat down, the dog sat with her. If Suzanne barn danced, the dog took a bathroom break and jumped in the van for a nap. Not a good plan!

Benny Jo definitely did not like to be in the crowds at the dance and did not like the music. She liked to be at the entrance just out of the way of heavy boots.

Maybe sitting on top of a big bale of hay would keep her out of the action. This was all Dan could think of to keep the little dog safe.

They would both sit upon a tall stack of bales near the door. Jim promised to help get the bales arranged. The Kingfisher police captain did not intend to alert the barn owners of his surveillance plan. It might not attract or draw the bank robber anyway, and was just one night of extra duty so if they caught someone in the car by accident it would just be an easy solution to the bank robbery.

The Kingfisher police captain talked with Dan and told him of the plan. He reasserted that the dog must be kept in the barn and not in the van. The police captain did not know how elusive the little dachshund could be. She could squirm out of anything. Suzanne wondered if Dan caged Benny Jo.

It was decided Jim would be in charge of parking all the vehicles. Dan was in charge of fixing a tall pillar of hay bales for him and the dog. He placed the stack near the door because he realized the dog hated the music and did not want to be stepped on.

Dan wished he could tell some of the others of their plan, but as promised, he kept mum. Nothing was to mar the police captain's plan if the felons showed up.

Benny Jo was the unknown factor that he vowed to control. The cycle group arrived safely just as the band was tuning up. Jim directed their parking while Dan piled the hay stack a little higher than usual for Benny Jo to sit upon.

Dan instructed Suzanne how to park her van as instructed by the police captain. He did not detect one soul in the parking lot that looked suspicious. Other vans came up and parked all around the spot allotted to Suzanne's van and everything looked okay to Dan and Jim. They convened at the door to meet before taking their places.

Jim really didn't want to be dancing, as he would miss all the action outdoors but, he couldn't act suspicious either. Jim offered to dog sit for a couple of dances whenever Dan wanted to square dance with the group.

Tobi drove Bart over to the square dance barn. He decided he would observe the action but would not be part of it. Tobi was going to let Bart do the dangerous parts, he was no dummy. Bart had created the problem and Bart would take all the dangerous action.

This was only fair and Bart was in complete agreement. Bart didn't want anyone to get in his way as he dug out the bagged money from the car wheel well.

Tobi parked his car in the very last row so he could make a fast getaway if need be. Bart carried a crow bar under his shirt which made him walk stiffly, but he didn't plan on dancing.

Tobi decided to enter the barn and listen until the dance had everyone inside and occupied with food, drink and dancing, before he approached the van. The bugs were out in full force, so bug spray was necessary. When Bart approached the car, Tobi silently drove his van far away to wait quietly up the road.

Tobi and Bart had decided not to hang out together. This was a caution that suited Tobi very well. He did not want to be part of a dangerous action in any way. If Bart was successful in getting the bank money, he was to fade back into a wooded area and wait for Tobi to pick him up.

It seemed to be the best plan to never be seen together or connected unless at a safe distance. Tobi had all their equipment packed up and ready to go if the plan succeeded. This was the best plan they had thought up.

If the dog barked or bothered Bart, all he had to do was knock her unconscious or be fast on the plunder of the van. When Bart glanced in the van it was empty and he still had the keys. He could not jump in and drive the van away because that would be too dangerous, so he planned to wait 45 minutes to an hour and enter the van when the dance was in full swing.

When everyone's attention was directed to the inside of the barn about 9:45 p.m., Bart signaled to Tobi he was going to open the car door and douse the light.

Benny Jo saw the car light go on from the top of her bed bales of hay and lept to the ground headed for the car. Just as she grabbed Bart's pant leg to bite, he struck her on the shoulder with his crowbar then started in to pry the wheel well open. As he reached for the bank bag, two policemen covered him with guns. Bart knew it was all over and it had all been a trap.

Down on his knees, face to the dirt, Bart felt his world slip out of control. The worst had finally happened and he was the lone fall guy for the bank robbery. No one else would be beside him in his jail cell. No friends would come up to share his misery and he had to stand alone.

Tobi did not earn any part in the bank robbery and Patty was left safe at home out of the way. He himself would have to pay the whole price of their failure. It was a disgusting thought and it didn't set well with him. Someone should have to suffer right along with him!

As the policeman put cuffs on him, then read his rights, Bart remained silent but he was thinking of a diabolical way to make the woman pay for this plan. He didn't doubt this was her way to get back at him for her kidnapping. That's what had occupied his thoughts as he rode along in the patrol car. He was formulating a wild story in his mind that would somehow involve her.

Tobi saw the whole fiasco from the top of the hill as Bart was arrested, cuffed, and driven away in the patrol car. It was good he was nowhere near the action and Tobi counted his lucky stars he was not in that patrol car being arrested with Bart. He only hoped Bart would keep his mouth shut and not involve anyone else! Somehow, he wasn't sure if Bart was that loyal of a friend to either Patty or himself.

Time will tell, he thought.

The little dog had been knocked unconscious by Bart's crowbar blow. Suzanne was brought out and driven with a second patrol car to the local vet hospital to treat the brave little dog. Everyone felt so bad that Benny Jo was hurt, but they were glad an arrest had finally been made. They were able to finally relax.

Chapter 11

Dan and Ellen rode in the police car with Suzanne and Benny Jo to the vet hospital in Hastings, Oklahoma. When Doc Barnes heard about the arrest of the bank robber and the bravery of the little dog, he was more than glad to help out. Benny Jo was a heroine, after all. She had taken the blow from the crowbar alongside her whole body, which was better than a blow to the head Bart had flung her to the side of the van. The barn dance had ended suddenly at 10:00 p.m. because of all the police vans and the arrest of the bank felon.

Everyone was stunned to think all the action was happening at their harmless barn dance. It was exciting to think everything would get back to normal, but the bike families were still worried about their two little guest bikers.

Would Suzanne need to head for home with her little dog and would Benny Jo survive the attack? The Kingfisher police captain informed the Duncan Police Captain of the arrest made that night out of courtesy for the help they gave.

Yes, the man who entered the van and pried the bank bags out of the wheel well had a scorpion tattoo on his right wrist. He also held the bank bag full of money when arrested. No doubt about it, this is the right guy.

The only disappointment was that he acted alone. If there was another person, no doubt they would be laying low. Of course, the Kingfisher police captain had everyone at the barn dance finger printed and photographed.

It was a miracle Tobi was so far away and out of all the action. It was a good plan for Tobi to be away from all the action so he could make a good getaway and escape all involvement.

Tobi thought to himself as he watched from his far away vantage point, *how fortunate am I, never to be involved with any of the capricious behavior of the two bank robbers?*

Suzanne was crying as they entered the vet hospital with Benny Jo. She carried the little dog carefully in her arms on her pillow so that no more harm could come to her little friend. If she had known what action was going to happen she would have tied the dog up, but that was wishful thinking.

No one could have predicted the actions of a little loyal dog. Benny Jo was carefully examined, x-rayed, and doctored then let sleep in a little dog bed. Suzanne wanted to stay with Benny Jo, but was assured everything was being done for the dog and she would be better fresh in the morning. A good night's rest was what they both needed. Thankfully, x-rays looked favorable for Benny Jo's recovery.

Bart was taken to the Kingfisher Police Station, finger printed, mug shots photographed, and placed in a bare cell. He was questioned for quite a while then he decided to lawyer up. It seemed they had a tight case against him, but he didn't want that crazy Kansas woman to go scot free.

If he was going to suffer, she was too! He was going to drag her through all the mud he could! Look at the trap she had helped set for him with her diabolical thinking! It would serve her right to be in prison just as he was. The thought that Patty would be alone only deepened his resentment against the Kansas woman.

Bart wondered what Tobi was doing now. Counting his lucky stars probably that he was well out of the way of police action. It was only justice that Tobi escaped detection, because he had not been in the bank heist from day one – only as the chauffer to the bank.

Patty had kept a little more of the money than he had actually given her, but she was entitled, he guessed. Bart had no animosity against those two, but since the bank knew a woman was involved in the robbery, Bart was going to make sure they thought of the Kansas woman. This would be the pay back for all the misery she had caused!

His questioning by the police captain in the evening was exhausting and he fell asleep immediately when placed in a cell bed. Bart ached all over the next day when he awoke. He had been served a good breakfast, much better than he was used to: bacon, eggs, and toast.

His lawyer was scheduled for a visit later in the morning and Bart planned how to play their game of information. Should he be reluctant to involve the woman instead of eager to blab it all out?

Suzanne had no thought about the bank robbers. Her concern was all for Benny Jo, her little pal. She was surprised the next day when the police captain called to ask her in for questioning.

Suzanne was really dumbfounded when she learned the bank robber implicated her in the bank heist. It was almost laughable but, it was scary to think of being punished because of his hatred of her. Someone who was so evil as to involve innocent people in their life of crime. The Kingfisher police captain was very under-standing and said this was just about what they expected the guy would claim.

The police captain had dealt with a lot of petty criminals, most would drag anyone down with them if they could. He was certain at least two more were in on the plan but, could not get Bart to implicate anyone else.

A bank heist had to have had a better escape plan than just randomly nabbing any car that showed up. Stranger things had a way of happening and the captain would play along in the game until Bart implicated other people.

Under several hours of questioning, Bart never broke down. They asked about the car he planned to get away in, "Where was it parked?"

He replied, "I was going to use the van because I had the keys to it."

This fact was the only true thing he said and could prove. The Kingfisher police captain talked with Suzanne's brother in Riverside, California and verified the facts Suzanne had said.

First she had accompanied him to Enid, Oklahoma in his van and was to drive it back to Arkansas City. Also, an extra set of keys was under the front seat of the driver's side.

The Kingfisher police captain wondered at the lies he heard Bart spout out about his involvement with Suzanne. It was almost ridiculous, but he let Bart rant on with his fantasy hoping he would trip himself up and involve his accomplices sooner or later.

The police captain sat with a sober face nodding at all the lies he was hearing. Two could play the game. One of Bart's fallacies was how much they both enjoyed barn dances and, in fact, had met at one the first time.

What an imagination this guy had, the captain thought. *Using every wild imagination he could to be believed!* With eyes wide and a smirk on his face, he pointed at the policeman and told him, "You ought to learn how to dance barn dance steps."

This was so ridiculous, a felon giving the police advice, Captain Jones almost smiled at the thought. "You won't be doing any barn dancing in jail, Sir, so think about that. Do you want all your other friends to escape punishment while you do time in jail, Sir?"

This made Bart stop and think. This was the time to implicate the Kansas woman further.

Her name was Suzanne, he remembered. "Suzanne thought this whole Kingfisher Bank plan up and contacted me to help her pull it off. She had her brother's car for our getaway. This was all her idea and the right time. Her brother was way off in California somewhere and she had his car to use. She came down to Kingfisher and picked me up."

Boy, could this guy spin a yarn, the captain thought. *He could cause all kinds of problems. Lawyers would have many lies to untangle and a hay day of a fight in court time.*

This crazy felon was going to be a headache for everyone! Bart had even begun to believe all the lies he was making up were true. He stated facts that seemed plausible, but were indeed ridiculous.

If anyone would listen to him, he would twist all the facts around to suit himself. His court appointed lawyer could not silence him. Bart wanted to be center stage all the time and interrupted all the proceedings at his arraignment.

He wanted Suzanne to be charged right along with him! What scum! The lawyer, Phil Smith, was truthful as he spoke to Bart.

"We are looking at some prison time for you, Bart. According to the facts the police captain has provided, you holding the bank bag in your hands is proof we cannot deny. All we can possibly hope for is a lenient sentence by the judge and possibly an early parole for good behavior on your part. Maybe if you cooperate truthfully with the court, it's possible you could have a lighter sentence," he said.

With that thought in his mind, Bart sat quietly thinking. *If he implicated the woman more fully, he would feel better, but would the court believe his story?*

Bart had to think and plot this all out. No one came to visit him, he was like a big "pariah" and toasted. No one wanted to be associated with him for fear of involvement in a bank robbery. Bart was sure he could con his court appointed lawyer into believing Suzanne was his real accomplice, but not the Duncan Police Captain. This fact he was fairly sure of. He was glad the case was in the Kingfisher County Court and maybe the Duncan Police would be kept out.

Suzanne was eager to see her little pet dachshund next morning as she pulled the van early into Hastings Vet Center. Doctor

Barnes met her at the door with Benny Jo in his arms, wide awake and bandaged up.

She looked so pitiful you could almost cry, Suzanne thought. She used her credit card to pay the vet doctor's bill and thanked him gratefully for the best of care. He even got up late at night to doctor her little pet dog.

What a guy, she thought!

If everyone in Oklahoma would act kindly as the vet doctor had, what a great state to be lost in. Breakfast called her back to camp, but Benny Jo was fasting after all the medications and didn't need any food yet. Back at Warika Park, breakfast smelled so good. Suzanne was glad she hadn't missed it. Fried potatoes, scrambled eggs, and ham casserole!

Benny Jo went back to sleep on her pillow in the van, still under medications. Since the arrest of Bart, everyone was relaxed and not worried about visiting with other campers. It was noted by the park guard those who left the grounds and went home.

Each name was given to the Kingfisher police captain to investigate. It was unfortunate Tobi's name was on the list and the vehicle license duly noted, but he did not plan on being anywhere near the Kingfisher Bank trial against Bart. Also, Tobi did not plan on visiting Bart and would caution Patty to stay away.

This was the safest way to stay out of Bart's trouble and just hope he kept his mouth shut. You could never know what to expect from Bart, you could just hope to remain anonymous.

Suzanne was asked to remain available if they had a court trial. She willingly gave the police captain all of her residential information. The Kingfisher police captain told her all about the fantastic lies Bart had informed him of and she was aghast at the audacity of his inventions. She thought a truthful person wouldn't stand a chance against his lies. Suzanne determined to enjoy a couple of days in Warika Park before driving on home.

She was glad the police captain didn't compound the van for evidence. He took a lot of pictures and finger prints and said that would be sufficient evidence for a trial if Bart wanted to plead innocent. Innocent!! Suzanne wondered how he could get away with that plea.

Innocent with a stolen bank bag full of money in his hands, then she remembered it was in her car. What other lies would Bart dream up to implicate her? Bart's lawyer wanted to talk to Suzanne to be certain if she had known Bart previously. Bart nixed that idea real quick. He wanted to keep his lawyer in the dark.

If the lawyer knew too much he would never believe Bart's story and that would be dangerous. Bart's inflated ego made him impossible to trust. The lawyer had dealt with many different criminal personalities and an inflated ego was one of the prominent signs that needed to be controlled. It always brought a stronger sentence down on the felon's head if he couldn't control his temper before the judge.

As Gary Smith, Bart's lawyer, explained this fact patiently to him he tended to listen. If he could portray a meek wounded personality in court, someone might believe his claim of partnership with Suzanne. Even the bank people knew there was a female involved in the bank robbery. Bart wondered if he could pull this off.

It was worth a try, he thought to himself, *and maybe she would suffer a little bit.*

Bart's lawyer did meet with Suzanne, however, and he was impressed with her honesty. All the facts she told him were perfectly in accord with the misadventure. She drove her brother to Enid in his car, then took the wrong turn south on the highway because of a cloudy day. Suzanne was not familiar with the car at first, but after traveling all week, she felt at ease in the car.

He even interviewed the dog pound attendant to verify the dog adoption and the check donation written on her account in the Arkansas City bank. The fact that she was totally responsible in all her money transactions weighed in as being an honest person. The lawyer was disgusted with all the lies Bart was trying to feed him, but he treated Bart with as much compassion as he would a child caught in many stories. Reasoning with Bart was like being in a duel with a devil.

Suddenly Bart became meek and quiet when questioned, as he decided it would get him more sympathy from his lawyer, as well as a judge or jury. He would play the part of a rejected friend or lover and maybe get a little sympathy from everyone. Bart was good at play acting and stringing people along.

At first, Bart's lawyer was puzzled by Bart's meek demeanor. An about face and change of mind signaled danger to the lawyer.

This man was really good at play acting, which made him more dangerous, he thought.

The lawyer could not figure out what had brought about this total character flip in his client and he became wary. Was the man planning suicide or did he have schizophrenia? The police captain duly noted the change of character on his chart.

The motorcycle friends decided to repeat some of the pleasures they had found relaxing at Warika. A five mile canoe trip was planned by the group with one pair staying at the park for camp guard duty.

Canoeing two people per boat took different muscles and gave each person'a good upper body workout. Luckily, Suzanne was invited to join. They were going to let her help row a boat to work out the arm and shoulder muscles.

Suzanne wondered about the dog. *Should she be in a canoe or would that be allowed?*

Everyone thought she would enjoy it and Suzanne put her in one canoe at her side. If Benny Jo jumped overboard, she would be left at camp. The least athletic couple begged to be camp attendants even though it was not their turn. Everyone teased Neal and Judy for being slackers. They mentioned the exercise would be a good workout for slack muscles. However, no one could convince Neal that he needed the muscle toning adventure. So it was decided they could be camp sitters during the day.

The group packed sandwich lunches, fruit, and water bottles to take along in little back packs and donned life vests for safety. At the end of the boat trip the crew would be bussed back to camp and boats would be trucked back. They were kind of glad they didn't have to paddle back up to camp making it a ten mile trip.

Of course, Benny Jo wanted to go on the canoe. All she had to do was drift along on the boat and bark at the birds. Suzanne started the first shift of paddling with Dan and Ellen.

The day promised to be a wonderful adventure. The canoes were easy and rowing was not hard work. It would be tiring later but, they would take turns and rest.

When it was Suzanne's turn to rest and just float along, she really enjoyed the scenery. Five miles did not seem to require a lot of work and she was thinking about early settlers who travelled the water ways to explore the country. They had to be very brave to settle in a land they had never known before. She wondered why they would travel so far away from one continent to another. Wanderlust?

They saw deer, badgers, lots of fish and little animals that scurried near the shore and sat up and peered at them. The squirrels were abundant. One thing she learned about their canoe, she had to move about carefully in it.

Their group landed on a sandy beach for lunching. They had pop, chips and cookies along with their sandwiches. Suzanne had brought a little ziplock bag of dog food along for Benny Jo. Water bottles stayed with the backpackers and all trash was kept to be brought back to camp and burned that night. The Warika camp people were very strict about keeping their camps clean.

Suzanne thought, *if I never learn anything else – I will be neat!!*

The people who wore scant clothing of shorts and shirts without cover got a sunburn on their knees and necks. They all arrived back at camp with scarfs tied around some places. Lucky for Suzanne, she had been warned to wear her cowboy hat tied under her chin to shadow her nose and neck.

Benny Jo just enjoyed all the scene and her brown hair covered her whole body well. Suzanne just hoped Benny Jo wouldn't get sunburned.

They were all glad they didn't have to row back home another five miles, however that night everyone felt they had used muscles they didn't know they even had.

Suzanne found a couple of pretty rocks for her collection. Supper was good, a big pot of ham and navy beans, corn bread, onions, and pickles. Her kind of food to enjoy. Paddling the boat had been fun. Something she had never tried before and it gave her a sense of accomplishment when done right.

The police captain came out to the Warkia Park camp to talk with Suzanne. At the arraignment, Bart claimed she was an accomplice and a partner in the Kingfisher Bank robbery. Of course, the police captain knew it was a false claim, but he wanted to be careful of the law and ask if she would come in to be interviewed about the bank robbery again.

Every point had to be covered by the district attorney to be sure of a fair trial. No one wanted to be accused of railroading a felon to jail without a fair hearing. He needed to cover all points of the law while prosecuting to make sure there was no prejudice or doubt of favoritism in this case.

Even the ridiculous claim of her involvement must be clarified as untrue. The district attorney wanted to be sure he had all his ducks in a row. Slippery felons would naturally create any trouble they could think up and this guy was the slickest he ever encountered. Bart was going to be a headache for everyone undoubtedly.

At first, he told the captain Suzanne thought up the whole caper and contacted him to help her out. She had promised him half of the money, then ran off with all of it!! The police captain wanted to make sure he could establish the fact that Bart had never encountered Suzanne before the bank robbery by questioning him about her home and her occupation before driving down to Kingfisher. He knew Bart only had facts he read in the newspaper about Suzanne, and the Harley motorcycle people of Miami, Oklahoma.

The police captain also realized the other participants in the bank robbery were wise enough to stay far away from Bart. There was nothing to gain and everything to lose by associating with him. The bank tellers could identify none of the participants because of the hoods they had worn.

All of the money Suzanne had spent had been taken from her bank account in the Arkansas City bank and she never flashed a lot of cash around that was not accounted for. Every check she had written was covered by her own money.

It was indecent that a thug like Bart could make up a bunch of lies about an innocent victim and have anyone believe him. It made their blood boil as the bikers and their wives heard about all the wild tales Bart was making up. He was really enjoying his celebrity status as he cornered anyone he could with his wide-eyed tales.

What a little faker! When asked to verify a statement or fact about his wild stories, he would clam up and pretend to be insulted they didn't believe him. His facts were so distorted, his lawyer warned him he was making a fool of himself by trying to implicate an innocent victim. He suggested Bart should just stick to true facts and admit his plan had gone awry.

One of the other cell mates taunted Bart with his idea that the other bank robber was enjoying spending his half of the stash away from any involvement of Bart's arrest.

Bart was taking the fall all by himself and someone else was getting off free. This did not set well with Bart, but he was not going to be goaded into a fight. It took all his will power to walk away from a fight with the crummy bum who was stuck in his cell just to irritate him. He really would like to punch his lights out, but restrained the impulse. He wondered if the guy was a stool pigeon.

The newspaper reporter was reprimanded by the Kingfisher police captain for aiding and abetting the bank robber with all kinds of information he would never have known had he not garnered it from the news. He would avidly read and enjoy all the notoriety he gained from their publications.

Vain people always needed a lot of attention and thrived on the news they read about themselves. When the reporter realized how he was helping a convict with all the notoriety, he quit writing anything about the Kingfisher Bank robbery. It made sense to him how he had been helping the criminal and boosting his ego up.

Maybe there was a saner way to publish news without stroking egos, he reasoned.

This approach, or course, dismayed Bart because he thrived on all the publicity he could get. His days became dull because everyone purposefully ignored him. No communication was the order of the day from the police captain.

The silent treatment was a real blow to Bart's pride because he thrived on all the attention he could garner. It frustrated him when everyone gave him the silent treatment and ignored his celebrity status. They treated him like he was just an ordinary inmate that they didn't want to hear from.

As everything got back to normal, the quieter the jail became which angered Bart. Being ignored every day ate at his pride, his ego was wounded. The police captain was sure this treatment would be a good way to really get at the truth and he wondered now how long it would take to undo Bart's ego.

He was good at the waiting game. Bart's lawyer was his only visitor now and he got all the flack. The lawyer didn't even argue with Bart now, he just sat, listened and took notes on his pad. Gary never tried to correct Bart even if he thought Bart was lying. He just sat and took notes and the taped interview for his case.

He did have compassion for the misguided fellow and all he could hope for was a light sentence and early release in his future with good behavior. His client seemed to be taking the fall for others, and loyally would not implicate his friends.

This was the only good fact he could garner but could not use in Bart's defense. Criminal loyalty was withholding criminal facts! What a predicament. The only good point Bart had went against him.

The police captain explained how Bart was using his relationship to Suzanne as a harassment plan to get back at her for all his imagined wrongs. Criminals had no morals and would use any situation to get back at other people.

Bart even made up false claims against his arresting officers. They wounded him by beating him unnecessarily. He had obtained a black eye from his fellow inmates in a grudge fight. Bart had then been placed in isolation because he irritated others talking too much.

Suzanne did not show up at his arraignment and this irritated Bart. He wanted her to hear all of his lurid accusations and be mad. There was no audience to play to and his arraignment didn't even have one court reporter. Bart was really puzzled at that kind of treatment. His star status was gone and it really was a big disappointment.

Bart could picture a big scene in his mind of photographers fighting over him to get pictures for all the big Oklahoma newspapers. No one! Absolutely no one showed up! In the court room it was just him, the district attorney and his lawyer, Gary Smith.

Bart went back to his cell quiet and humiliated. The cold facts closed in on him in his cell. He was a nobody! A punk criminal caught in the act of retrieving bank money he himself had lost by his own stupid – stupid – stupid actions. Suzanne called her brother with news she heard from the police captain.

The judge would not grant bail for the bank robber to be released because he was too much a flight risk. The police had captured him with great effort and he was too slippery to let go free again before trial.

Bart got better meals while in jail and a warm place to sleep even if he did feel his ego was abused. He wouldn't try to fight it, free meals and he had plenty of room for recreation.

Phil and Frankie were about ready to start home, so Suzanne asked the Kingfisher police captain if she could go back home to Kansas. She wanted to put Phil's car back and exchange it for her own when they went to trial.

The statements had all been recorded of her kidnapping and escape from the road park on Highway 81. The attendant at the gas station who had sold her gas and four candy bars was interviewed.

He corroborated all her facts. She paid for her gas with a bank card issued from her Arkansas City bank. Her purchases were all within normal range and Suzanne carefully budgeted her income and covered all expenses carefully.

Not a personality that would hook up with a bank robber, the captain thought.

While things quieted down at the jail and became dull the cycle group was still relaxing at Warika Park. They had enjoyed each day at the park and were preparing to cycle on North toward Alabaster Caverns State Park.

Suzanne decided she had better get back home and rest up before Phil and Frankie returned. Maybe the garden needed a little weeding since she had been gone almost twelve days. It was a nice time of rest, but home was calling her back.

The cycle group decided to accompany Suzanne to the Kansas Oklahoma state line and see that she was on the way home north from Enid, Oklahoma once again. It would be a long drive north, but they would all take it easy and stop often to rest for meals and coffee breaks.

Everyone wanted to be fresh and in good shape on the road. This meant careful planning and safety for everyone. They were never in a rush to jump from one town to another, but stopped to enjoy meals, coffee breaks, bathroom breaks, and shopping fun. If there was an interesting antique store, they stopped for another break to look. You never knew what kind of treasure you might find just looking over antiques nobody else wanted.

Suzanne and Benny Jo enjoyed that kind of travel too, unhurried and pleasurable – stopping in every other town for refreshments of some kind. The city parks were always inviting for travelers.

When the group finally arrived at Enid, Suzanne had talked herself into a one day trip to see the Alabaster Caverns. It was only a jog straight west toward Freedom, Oklahoma and she had never visited the Alabaster Caverns. One of the small rooms was described like being inside a beautiful pearl with all white walls.

One of the cycle families had found the small cavern which was not open to the public and was close to the highway on private property unattended. It was easy to drop into and climb out of like a cellar. The inside was exquisite and there were no signs to prohibit their visit. The actual Alabaster Park entry was further away to the west and separate from the little farm cave.

The cave extended further than anyone had ever explored or mapped. It might have even extended clear up through Kansas to Hutchison. No one knew. The cycle group would visit the Alabaster

State Park proper the next day as they planned to stay overnight in a motel in Enid. Everyone was dusty and ready for a good night's rest in a real bed. From the very most Southern part of Oklahoma to the Northern line was a long, hot dusty ride on a cycle.

A good steak supper cooked by the restaurant chef would be welcomed by the Harley cooks. While at lunch, the group discussed the Great Salt Plains State Park area at Jet, Oklahoma. That their state was full of salt and that they actually walked over it was an astounding fact.

The dirt was white and there was a lake to water ski around or swim. Or course, sunburn would be much more painful because of the salt. Just to think the Arkansas River that framed her hometown also flowed through the Great Salt Plains in Oklahoma. Just to think an underground salt mine linked the two states, Kansas and Oklahoma.

Suzanne imagined they were the salt of the earth in the Americas. Kansas and Oklahoma contained great treasures both underground and above.

Suzanne had always been proud of her state, but now she included her sister state, Oklahoma. Other states might have proud things to enjoy, but Oklahoma and Kansas could hold their own with underground salt mines and beautiful caves.

Benny Jo enjoyed a few chunks of good steak along with her small portion of dry dog food. She was well satisfied at days end in a little motel cabin that actually allowed pets to visit. Of course, she loved her little dog bed in the van, but her real aim was to protect Suzanne even though she snored loudly at night. The dog tolerated this just to be near. She needed family to feel loved deep down in her little doggy heart.

Phil and Frankie were taking a few extra days of vacation before returning home. They planned to visit the Redwood Forest area in Northern California, so they began a leisurely drive up along the coast. Suzanne told Phil she planned to be available for the bank robber's trial as a witness when and if they needed her. She was troubled that Bart was lying about her involvement in his escapade. He could gain nothing by lying for his friend.

She couldn't imagine what his story could do to help in his own predicament. She wondered if he was just trying to shelter the woman from being prosecuted, of course, he would not give out the names of those who helped plan the Kingfisher Bank robbery. Bart thought he was being noble by using Suzanne to protect his female friend. How clever they all were to remain away from involvement and let Bart take all the punishment!

The Kingfisher police captain searched through all the school records in Oklahoma to find any information concerning Bart's education, family, friends, and town birth records. It was a long exhausting search and he came up with few facts.

The other female felon was well-protected if Bart wouldn't give out her name. The district attorney had to prove Suzanne was not his accomplice. Her record in Kansas was solid and her employment and bank record reflected a life dedicated to hard work and achievement. Bart, on the other and, had scanty employment records and never held a steady job at any time in his life!

The first day of Bart's trial was a nightmare. Suzanne had returned her brother's car safely to his garage and exchanged all of her paraphernalia to her beat up older van. The Harley cycle group had directed her back north on the proper highway toward home, so she couldn't get lost again. Suzanne could easily find her way up and down the Chisholm Trail Highway 81 to Kingfisher now without any trouble.

She knew she was not going to enjoy the Oklahoma bank robber's trial, however. It was a miracle she had not been killed. She was grateful God had protected her life. Maybe she was here for a greater purpose than she was aware of. Suzanne had to learn compassion for others and the Harley cycle group had taught her a lot about compassion. Poor Bart, he was alone now in his jail cell and she wondered what kind of sentence he would be given to serve. *Why did he blame her for all his troubles?*

Suzanne wondered if Bart had any family who might really care about his soul. In the courtroom, Bart really looked forlorn and sad. If he was putting on an act, he was good at it. He looked around at the audience to see if he could recognize anyone and settled down with a sigh like an abandoned waif when no one came to his aide. After observing the dual personality change, the district attorney was not fooled.

Bart's lawyer just hoped for a light sentence and maybe his client would remain docile through his whole procedure and give a good impression of his character. Maybe. The lawyer kept his fingers crossed. He really didn't feel at ease with his client's abrupt character change.

Everyone rose respectfully when the judge arrived. The jury was already chosen and the lawyer had called Suzanne to drive down to Kingfisher. First, he had the bank tellers on the witness stand to testify. It went against his case that they could not identify the woman accomplice because of her head gear and mask. The color of her hair was tan and her height and weight average. It could have been anyone.

The bank head cashier verified the woman had pocketed a lot of cash in high dollar amounts that were not retrieved in the bank bag. This gave Bart a jolt that Patty had kept a lot of cash he didn't know about and he thought she had very little. Now he knew there was a lot more in her bag, plus she had suckered $300 more from him.

No family member came to back Bart up. This was sad, but Bart had not expected anyone to be there for him. Bart didn't understand family loyalty because he hadn't cared about anyone as he grew up. His own mother had annoyed him with all her preaching at him. She had so many rules, he was never going to try to please anyone but himself. He never took any of her advice - from day one - and greed drove him. He never learned from any of his mistakes!

Bart had nothing but contempt for his whole court procedure. First, they would pronounce him guilty then give him a stiff sentence to serve in jail. Then, if he was real polite and good, they might cut off some of the time he was supposed to serve then kick him out of jail.

He would not have a job or any way to get money and he already figured he would have to rob another bank! His future did not look very bright. A counselor at the Kingfisher jail had visited with him about his future one day and tried to cheer him up. While incarcerated, they would offer him schooling to fit him for a good job in several different areas of interest.

He could choose to study for an interesting vocation that he might be good at. Ho ho! Back to school again, if he wanted to learn. Bart thought about this counsellor and he couldn't figure out why anyone would want to help him learn anything. He really didn't want to slave away at some boring occupation day after day for peanuts. While in jail he could either work or lay in his bunk and stew. Anyway, the counsellor was giving him something to think about and information about the available schooling offered to inmates. Bart wondered why anyone would care about all those losers in jail.

They called it "rehab". Bunk! It looked like slave labor to him, but lounging around in a four by four bunk room jail looked awful too! The trial was a joke as far as he was concerned. They all knew he was guilty when he picked up the bank bag out of the woman's van. The only doubt he could inject was against the Kansas woman.

The prosecution case was cut and dried. The bank robber was the only one who knew where the money was hidden and he proved that properly. The real battle would be over the innocence of the Kansas woman and how she became involved.

Bart had no car registered in his name and Tobi never came forward to clear up that issue. He would have been foolish to have become involved. Bart thought he could still get revenge against Suzanne.

Somehow her story really impressed Bart's lawyer as being true. He could not break the thought in his mind that his client was really out for revenge. Still he had to give a fair deal to Bart who trusted him to be on his side. The lawyer carefully made up his defense.

Bart came from a broken home, further didn't graduate from high school. His education stopped at 9th grade so he was not proficient enough for a good job, but given a chance might do better. Life had not been good for him. His mother could not provide luxuries for him with the scant income she raised him on. His father left the family early, disappeared and never helped with any resources. It was a sad tale and his lawyer had to drag out a little sympathy for Bart with this narration.

The judge had heard the same defense story countless times in many cases. Mom was always left with the youngster to raise alone and dad always beat it, when and if, a baby appeared. Sometimes the kid resented what happened and turned to crime, but good schooling seemed to be the key to success.

If someone really wanted to learn, Oklahoma would make education available in or out of jail. That is one key plan that was good for everyone. Of course, there were many single parent families who succeeded and never got into any trouble with the law.

These people became successful and the judge wished he knew why they were so blessed and why some of the others were turned to crime instead. Dropping out of school early was one key factor. The more education a child went after, the better. Of course, some folks continued to learn well after dropping out of school, especially if they were interested in their vocation.

If Bart presented himself in a contrite, truthful manner, accepting punishment for his greed, the judge considered being lenient with his sentence. Maybe lightening the time with good behavior a little. This all depended on Bart. However, the fact that all of the bank money was not recovered was still against Bart.

Recovering more of the Kingfisher Bank money would have helped the judge to be more lenient, but Bart would not give out any information about what happened to the other money.

When Suzanne was on the witness stand giving her account of the abduction, Bart put a frown on his face and pretended to be astonished. The only question his lawyer asked her was if she had ever been in Enid, Oklahoma before.

It was a good one, because she had been to Enid many times while travelling, but it was her first time in Kingfisher. Most of her travels in Oklahoma had been through Tulsa or Oklahoma City. The lawyer had found out Suzanne was raised in Oklahoma City and educated there. This made a good point, but could be for both sides. Good education produced good stock.

Bart's lawyer left the good point for the jury to ponder and decide. He did not try to make her seem devious. Although he did make the point she was better educated than Bart. Bart was furious that his own lawyer made him look childish and uneducated to the jurors.

He wanted to be built up in stature, but made to be the scape-goat by others bravely taking their punishment! Not stupid! Bart could barely restrain himself from jumping up and screaming at his lawyer. He immediately saw that screaming at his own lawyer and creating a tantrum in court would go against the image of a weak and helpless creature he was trying to portray to the jurors. Bart just gritted his teeth and closed his eyes. The district attorney noted how uncomfortable this speech made Bart, however, and he wondered how long it would be before Bart lost his barely controlled temper.

He let Bart's lawyer ramble on about his poor education and indigent family and all the poverty Bart endured. Bart wanted to be on that witness stand explaining things himself, but his lawyer nixed that idea from the very beginning. Bart understood this was the lawyer's big show.

His little court appointed lawyer, Gary Smith, wasn't doing a bad job in his narration. He had to give the guy credit for all the good points he brought out in favor of Bart. Lack of education, lack of income, and an unstable family.

Where was my mother? Bart wondered to himself. *She didn't show up in court to back me up!*

Then again, he never bothered to visit her either, so maybe she was unaware of his predicament. After all the newspaper stories and pictures, she surely had seen his face in the news! Maybe his mother was so ashamed she couldn't face him at all.

Well, there went his last prop. Bart was really down and out. When mothers failed you, it was just the last straw and he had nothing else to hang on to now. Bart realized he was really alone and must somehow pull himself up and out of his own mess.

Before, his mom had always paid the fine for his mess up but, now she remained aloof and away. Not one visit had she made to the jail he was locked in! Or course, this was one caper she could never buy him out of. His mother would have been the one witness in his favor in court but she had not come to visit him and did not offer any assistance to his lawyer.

The district attorney used that sad thought in his speech against Bart. His mom had given up on him. Her other actions to buy him out of his felonies did not set well with the jurors and the district attorney dwelt on the fact that Bart's own mother did not appear in his defense!

When the district attorney had Suzanne on the stand, he helped her paint a sterling character. She was a reliable person, a trusted employee with a good job, who had earned vacation time. She had built up retirement funds and had a good savings account.

This all went to her credit and made Bart look bad. Bart was trying to make her look like a criminal who was crazy for money but the accusations just didn't fit. This was why Bart's lawyer would not put him on the witness stand. He could not stick with the truth and would not be reliable in cross examination. Gary Smith knew he was defending a ticking time bomb!

Bart was trying to incriminate Suzanne with his bank robbery in any way he could imagine. Although she had never been accused by the police, Bart was trying hard to convince everyone that she was an accomplice. Bart's lawyer had been allowed to visit and question her as he made his case for leniency for Bart before the trial and he did not want to use her in Bart's defense.

This only made Bart look better in the lawyer's opinion and the judge might consider his point to give Bart a lighter sentence.

If Bart would remain silent and not burst into one of his tirades against Suzanne he would look better in front of a jury, Gary thought. *More gentlemanly.*

Bart was only thinking of revenge! He did not have the mental capacity to think beyond this point. Bart wanted revenge on someone for being set up and caught with the bank bag in his possession.

Bart thought this was all Suzanne's plan against him and he really didn't know the Kingfisher police captain had planned this all on his own. It would not have mattered to him anyway as he was beyond reason.

His stay in prison had only alienated him from everyone. The prison psychiatrist gave him all the schooling information offered in the prison as well as the planned recreation of games offered the inmates. He was trying to make Bart have a hopeful outlook about prison time. It was surely the place where he would wind up.

He found Bart in a bad mood the first day of the trial, which had gone against him. The worst fact was the district attorney using his own mother against him! She was the one person who always stood up for him, but now she didn't even show up. His lawyer suggested perhaps Bart could talk to her. Bart wasn't even sure he remembered the phone number.

This was a pitiful point, the lawyer thought.

Neglect, it was a discouraging point to Gary Smith. Not one was in Bart's favor. The judge and jury would surely hold that point against his client. What good point could he bring out in favor for his client the next day?

Suzanne remembered the name of Bart's woman friend during the caper - *Patty.* Not a last name, just a first name. Gary Smith asked Bart if he had a friend named Patty.

Bart denied knowing anyone by that name. His lawyer was sure that was a lie. He could not bring any information out about Patty until Bart actually acknowledged her name. Patty was a common shortening for the name of Patricia, but there were too many to try and make a connection.

The fact that Bart denied knowing a "Patty" made the lawyer know he was not going to get any information about her, even if she had lots of the bank money that was still unaccounted for.

Suzanne told the court people how she escaped from Bart and Patty. She spoke of how she had been in the woman's restroom while Bart was outside the building then Patty shoved her out the door. Bart, clad in his stocking cap, pushed her in the driver's seat of her car and then went to the back of the van while Patty was still in the women's restroom.

Bart was very surprised and chased the van up to the highway, but she was going full speed and out ran him. The shopkeeper ten miles down the road verified her visit to get gas, the four candy bars and an Oklahoma map.

Also, she had informed him that a felon might be walking his way from a park.

If there had ever been a doubt in anyone's mind, they had to believe the store owner because he observed that Suzanne seemed very nervous and jerky in the way she stammered out the information.

The fact that she drove straight to the Duncan police with her story also made an impression on the jury. This is what anyone would have been expected to do. Bart's lawyer asked him later what he first did when left at the park to walk without a vehicle. Bart laughed and said they had it all planned that way.

He sent a friend to pick him up. His lawyer jumped carefully on this information of a good friend who would pick Bart up on the highway. Bart lied and said he didn't know the friend she had sent. It was someone who was a special friend of Suzanne's.

Gary knew he was hearing another fib, but he controlled his anger. It must have been the getaway car that missed the actual bank robbery! Now that he knew his client was a skillful liar, he felt he could not represent him fairly. He asked Bart to provide a description of the friend and of the car.

Gary informed the police captain of his intent to refuse the case. When asked the real reason, he merely said he had no case. There was nothing to beg for mercy with and everyone already knew his client was guilty of bank robbery.

The judge decided the lawyer must present the best defense he could with what Bart had already told him. He would not be excused from the case because it would make the felon look worse than he already did.

Gary told the judge Bart wanted on the witness stand and it would be a disaster for his case. It never went well when people tried to defend their actions in court because most criminals believed they were right and twisted facts to suit themselves. He was not excused from the case.

Gary decided to play on the jury's emotion when it came time for his summary. He would remind the jury Bart had no friends to support him and no family that most young people had to rely on. His friend (whoever he was) had disappeared and left him to stumble alone. The one friend who picked him up on the highway never acknowledged him here in his court trial or his jail cell.

How do you make a case of defense on a pack of lies? the lawyer sighed to himself.

He wondered if Bart confided any information to a cell mate. The only good thing Suzanne had to say in Bart's defense was she was glad he hadn't shot her and tossed her in the Canadian River. This had worried her at the time they drove past all the signs on the road.

The fact that he had not physically harmed her was one good point in his favor. The fact that he protected the identity of the other female was frustrating but compassionate. It was commendable that Bart wasn't bothered with her being free to spend the other $15,000 or $20,000.

Bart planned to visit his two friends when his jail time was up, however. He wanted to know what Patty had done with the bank money in her possession. Not that he claimed any of it, he would just be curious.

The fact that Patty was smart enough to hide that amount in her handbag and hang onto it in that roadside restroom was a good thought. Bart had to admit, Patty wasn't as dumb as he thought! Staying completely away from his trial was smart, too.

Bart knew Tobi was not going to come forward as his friend. It would be too dangerous for him. They were both doing exactly as he would have done in the same circumstance. Lay low!

Bart sighed. The guy in the next cell had cried all night long and kept him awake. He must have been real young and stupid to be locked up at his age.

Sleeping in jail was like trying to sleep in a hospital with disruptions and guard inspections going on all night. The prison parson came to visit one or two days each week.

Bart wondered, *why anyone would want to bother with a bunch of low life criminals? Did the parson think anyone would take him seriously and tell him all their troubles?*

Bart just sat, listened and agreed with him every time he showed up. Bart wondered why anyone would care, but maybe he was paid a good salary for his visits.

Bart thought, *what a way to make a living. Just visit all the junkies in jail then report all the information they told you to the warden. Maybe one day you would hit a jackpot!*

Bart was so cynical he was hard to reach. He never had a trusted friend before in his life! Bart did ask the parson to talk to his mother. He really wanted her on his side.

It was a sad thing for the parson to see. Bart had to rely on a stranger to visit his own mother and see why she wouldn't come to the jail to visit her only child. If there was an illness or something, he could handle that, but total rejection the parson could not understand. Still he promised to contact Bart's mom to see if she was okay.

The prison minister made an appointment to visit with Bart's mom at her convenience. He understood her schedule was full to the brim trying to make a living at two underpaid jobs with no healthcare insurance or any hope of a retirement plan in place.

The hope of an only child to help while retired was not in her favor. Bart never gave her any sense of achievement either. The prison minister wondered if she was a Christian mother who tried to bring up a wayward child.

When he visited her she seemed to be tired and defeated. One reason being a son who turned out to be a total failure. If all her efforts had been derailed at every point, her success was a sure defeat. Evidently, she had tried to counsel and raise Bart all alone with no help from Bart's relatives or any church for guidance. The minister wondered if any of her friends had invited her into a church. Well, he would!

He gave her a program of all the activities of his own church and explained all the programs that would be offered Bart during his jail time. If Bart wanted more education, he could complete his schooling and earn a GED. Also, Bart would learn a good trade of his own choosing with top-notch teachers. It was a good thing if Bart wanted to apply himself. The minister left Bart's mom with a hopeful feeling but she knew her son would have to take the first step of obedience.

She still did not go to visit him in his prison cell. She told the minister she felt like she was Bart's weak link to crime. She needed to sever his crutch of dependence and his need to blame everyone else for his condition. Bart needed to grow up and mature. He could not be a baby forever. The minister agreed.

The minister felt they had a good visit and his mother knew now she was a weak link into his life of crime. She still needed guidance though, so the prison minister put her on his personal prayer list.

He told Bart of his visit and relayed the message of his mom's exhaustion from overworking herself with two different jobs.

The minister hoped Bart could find a little compassion for others in his character. This was a new thought for Bart to consider and he left him with it. The prison minister also visited with Bart's lawyer, Gary Smith, to tell him the reason Bart's mom was absent from the trial proceedings.

It was natural that she was working day and night at two jobs with hardly any time off. Money was scarce and she did not lead a luxurious life. She never neglected Bart and he had in fact only visited his mother when he needed money or food. Bart was still a baby adult. The lawyer wondered what it would take to make Bart grow up! He was still disgusted!

The lawyer decided to enlighten Bart with his real feelings and come clean about his disgust.

"I don't like you personally, Bart, but I am committed to represent you in court in the best possible defense we can assemble together. I know you have been feeding me lies about all your actions during this bank robbery. It has hampered any defense I could produce for the jury to consider leniency in your sentencing. You have tried to protect the ones who helped with this bank robbery and you have tried to accuse an innocent woman that you kidnapped for an escape with the money. I cannot keep you from serving some time in jail for this crime, but if I can present true facts for the jury to consider, it will all be to your favor. If you do not stick with true facts, it will be to your disadvantage and I will not be a party to untrue facts nor present them in court."

With that speech said, his lawyer took his notes and left the jail visiting block. Bart sat thinking. His lawyer saw right through him!

If Bart thought his lawyer would join in and support him with all his lies he was mistaken. The error in his presumption was money fed his lawyers aims. That the lawyer would do or say anything Bart told him to for the money. Still he had to admire the man for telling him straight facts. Bart was impressed with the prison minister, too. The parson had actually gone and visited his mother.

It was comforting for Bart to realize his mother worked hard at two low paying jobs just to exist. Bart had never given a thought to anyone but himself in his whole entire life before. She had a reason for staying home from all her labor. This made Bart feel a little better now.

It was a new notion to think of someone other than himself or to understand their physical need. His mother was the only person in the whole world he trusted or ever leaned on.

Being a prison minister sometimes meant working with the whole family of the one being incarcerated, comforting and ministering to whole families parted by crime. It was an exhausting task sometimes to try and help people withstand trials they were going through. He had to help them handle angry feelings of despair.

If he could not comfort them with the hope that God still loved them, he experienced defeat. It took a lot of prayer time and patience to know how to give help from the Lord God. Proper help.

Suzanne wanted nothing more than to go home and settle Benny Jo into her new little space but, she was still needed at the Kingfisher trial. More than one day was needed to reveal all the important facts: missing money and missing witnesses. Who was the other missing woman and what were the means of escape from the roadside park?

The jury was not fooled because the district attorney had brought out the fact that Bart had been rescued by someone and taken home from the roadside park. He was then brought back to Warika Park to be included in an invitation to the barn dance at Hastings. The fact of missing money still in possession of someone else was the main factor against Bart! The fact Bart did not own a car was also important.

Suzanne decided to leave Benny Jo with a friend while she testified in Kingfisher. The little dog didn't need to be there and had not completely healed from her broken rib. Suzanne knew the dog still hurt if she tried to pick her up. She did help Benny Jo out of the car and up and down steps.

The Harley cycle friends finally wound up their vacation and went home to rest up. They had experienced more fun and danger on this trip than they ever had on any previous occasion. They had made a lasting friendship with Suzanne and Benny Jo. Many pictures were being processed and would be shared over the year. Even back home in Miami, Oklahoma people had read of their part in the capture of the Kingfisher bank robber.

They received a lot of congratulations they felt they did not deserve. Everyone in Miami seemed to know Danny and Jim were the heroes of the group. One reporter had heard Dan speak about watching over the dog on the bales of hay and how she escaped when she heard the car door open. When they heard Benny Jo had been bashed alongside her body with a crowbar by the bank robber, all the dog lovers in Miami, Oklahoma were mad.

It's a good thing the Miami people would not be on the jury because they all thought beating a little dachshund dog made Bart look twice as bad. If the dog would have been used as evidence of the crime, Bart wouldn't have had any leniency.

While this point would not be allowed in the court trial, the Miami news reporter made sure it was in his newspaper account. He was a dog lover! Bart's lawyer read all the Oklahoma newspaper accounts each day to know what he was up against.

He hoped nobody else read the Miami, Oklahoma newspaper. Bart admitted he had reacted out of fear instead of wisdom. It was too bad for the dog he had not thought to bring along a dog bone to quiet her down.

One mistake after another – the story of his life. The preacher wanted Bart to reform and go straight, get back in school and learn a trade.

Maybe it's too late for me, he thought.

Actually some of the inmates in the Oklahoma prison were there because of drugs. Some were so wounded by drug use they would never recover and be normal. The prison minister wondered what the State could do about rehab. Some had hope, but not all.

Only prayers could help to rebuild those beyond the human capacity. If a life could be rebuilt and become productive maybe Bart could grasp the possibility.

Bart's mom decided to send him encouraging letters once she got a hold of his address. She thought the prison would be way off in another town and it would be an expensive long trip to travel with time off from work.

How would I ever be able to get there? she thought.

It was another thing to worry about but, she would do every thing she was able to do for Bart. The prison minister mentioned prayer was very effective and God was able to help her encourage Bart.

This was a peaceful thought for his mom. She was not alone and God would help her. The prison minister had been able to give her a lot of encouraging information about prison educational programs offered to inmates. Prayer was the more productive action anyone could take on Bart's behalf.

Suzanne knew her way up and down the Chisholm Trail. She was not going to get lost again in Oklahoma! It was really funny now that she thought about it. The road was so plainly marked.

The district attorney kept asking the lawyer to find the woman named Patty. He was sure she would know where the rest of the Kingfisher Bank money was.

If Bart was ever going to be truthful, it might have been to the lawyer. It was strange the man was so protective of her identity, but was so vindictive toward his kidnapped victim. Someone had accompanied Bart to the barn dances and to Warika Park.

The district attorney was still scouring all the evidence of those registered at the park: their employment, addresses, and character references. It took a lot of time, but he hoped it might yield some references to the missing friend.

Nobody registered at Warika Park was named Patty or Patricia. Bart had not registered his name at the park either, but he would have had to be there to know about the two barn dance invitations and see the Harley people driving off to the dances. Maybe Patty was hiding out and protecting her own identity because of the money she had taken. The district attorney was searching only for two men, one with a car for transportation.

Only one man had registered at Warika Park on a moped bike – that had to be Bart! Where had be bought the vehicle? Want ads were researched in all the towns up and down the Chisholm Trail. The moped trail search led to one town: Chickasha, Oklahoma.

The ad's date was identified to be just before the adventure in Warika. The person who sold the moped did not know Bart and had only received cash. Bart had been using an unrenewed license. The guy selling the moped seemed innocent and above board. He was not acquainted with Bart or Patty.

"The other accomplices must reside in the same town Bart's mom resided," the district attorney decided

He made a dedicated research through all the school records in Duncan. The Kingfisher district attorney had the help of the Duncan police captain when searching for Patty using every Stephen's County record the Duncan police captain could get hold of. The sixth grade Duncan drop out didn't have any friends to speak of. He had been a loner so it was discouraging.

One of Bart's cell mates taunted Bart with his idea that his girlfriend had used part of the cash to buy a car to head for Mexico or Canada for an easy life free from care. This was exactly what Patty had done, in fact, and was on her way to Canada for a new life free from all past crime.

Of course, the inmate didn't know this for sure but, it was what he would have done himself. Bart really didn't care what Patty did, as he was through with her anyway.

against his lawyer's advice, Bart still wanted to defend himself in court and present his own version of the bank heist. The lawyer would not agree figuring Bart would end up with a larger sentence and no sympathy whatever from a jury because of his personality.

Gary Smith had no sympathy for Bart and he figured the jury would not either. It was a touchy situation because Bart didn't understand why he couldn't gain sympathy by telling lies. It would be a disaster if he jumped up and demanded to be heard.

It was all about being the "star" of his own show. If the lawyer wasn't fooled, much less would anyone else be fooled. When it came time to present Bart's case and ask for leniency, Gary wondered if Bart could keep still and not cause a problem.

The only good point Gary Smith could prove was he did not shoot at the car as Suzanne drove away. Not very substantial but, would it gain favor for Bart? The bank president really wanted to know the name of the other felon and put pressure on the Kingfisher police captain to give Bart a third degree questioning. He was a hard nut to crack as he just stared blankly at the wall and never budged.

Both borders north and south had been alerted to be on the lookout for an Oklahoma car with someone named Patty driving it. Canada called first and sent information to the Kingfisher Police of one Oklahoma car with a driver named Patty Long crossing their border early one morning. Her license was issued in Stephen's County and she fit a lot of the descriptions given by the police captain.

Suzanne could not identify her perfectly because of her make-up and dyed hair. The police captain asked the Canadian official if he could search for the missing $20,000 bank notes.

Most people travelling carried extra monies and it would not be out of place for one to have extra bank notes, the Canadian guard observed.

The Kingfisher captain asked if he had the power to hold anyone for questioning. The touchy situation for both officials was whether to let Patty go safely across into Canada or detain and search her car for stolen money. She had never been proven guilty of any crime so the Canadian official was inclined to let her be. The Kingfisher police captain had his hands tied. At least he had one name to research and see if there was a connection to Bart.

The fact that Patty Long had recently bought the car and paid cash for it from the car lot in Duncan, Oklahoma, gave the captain hope. The fact that she was already out of the country was bad news to give the bank president. He considered her a lost cause. The fact Patty had just purchased the car meant someone else had to be driving Bart around on his adventures to the Warika Park.

He went over his name list. Four names were considered interesting to research. None of them acknowledged being acquainted with Bart Ellis and why would they? A smart accomplice would never own up to friendship with a bank robber who was accused of taking $120,000. Everything frustrated the Kingfisher police captain's efforts, but Bart's mother identified the one name she knew had been a contact of her son.

He was employed and lived a quiet life but he was an acquaintance even though he was reluctant to admit it. When questioned by the Kingfisher Police he explained he didn't want to acknowledge Bart because of the trouble he was now in. Also, they were not really close friends, just acquaintances. The police captain wondered if he could connect Tobi Benton to the woman, Patty Long.

Of course he would have to be careful about his questions. Bingo, here was the owner of the transport car to Warika Park and maybe the barn dances! The police captain very carefully phrased his questions.

Had Tobi Benton used the recreation programs offered at Warika? Fishing had been his main outdoor recreation and point of interest.

He did admit going to the first barn dance but claimed to have stayed at Warika during the second barn dance. Bart would have needed transport someway to both barn dances and the moped did not show up at either one.

Tobi had used his correct name when registering at Warika Park, which was to his credit. The coincidence of his friendship with Bart was against him, however. The police captain put an undercover surveillance detail on Tobi just to track his actions and habits during the trial.

He scanned the van licenses to see if Tobi had driven his car to both barn dances. It was registered as entering and not being present at the second barn dance at Hastings. More police surveillance was at the Hastings, Oklahoma barn dance site so it was hard to evade notice there. The police captain wondered why Tobi would show up then leave the dance. It could only mean one thing.

Tobi had delivered Bart to the Hastings farmer's barn, then left to be out of the police action to wait and pick up Bart when he had the money in his possession! It was a good thing the King-fisher police captain had set his trap for the felon. It was their last chance to apprehend the criminals.

The police captain was not going to let Tobi Benton escape scot free from his involvement in aiding and abetting a criminal act. He began to put pressure on Tobi. His was the vehicle that transported Bart and Patty to Kingfisher Bank.

His was the vehicle that transported Bart to the barn dance, the captain was sure of it! Some of his officers were sent with the express reason to find tire tracks to put Tobi's car close by the barn for surveillance. The trees on one hill yielded this evidence so the captain had Tobi Benton arrested as an accomplice. Now the only one to escape needed to be identified and the captain was sure it was Patty Long.

He would have to convince the Canadian official to keep her under surveillance! Patty was trying to find employment, which meant she intended to stay in Canada. The Canadian police had no trouble keeping track of Patty. She settled down to wait tables at a small restaurant and had found a room in a nearby boarding house. Not one to rock the boat, Patty was being conservative and laying low.

When Tobi was arrested and charged as an accomplice in the bank heist, he was put in a separate room from Bart. The captain did not want them together for obvious reasons.

The captain wanted to know why Tobi didn't show up at the bank on time to pick up Bart and the woman. Tobi did not acknowledge being present at the bank, and it frustrated the police captain. Tobi obviously went to Warika Park and the Hastings barn dance with Bart.

When searching Tobi's car, they found physical evidence Bart was in it eating hot dogs. The car was trashed with napkins and never cleaned up. The captain thought these two were not very wise at hiding their involvement. It just made his case a little more solid against Tobi.

It seemed Patty Long was the most careful of the three and smartest to flee to Canada with $20,000 of the money in her bag. Tobi claimed the woman parked in front of Kingfisher Bank was innocent and just happened to be in the wrong spot, but he never claimed to drive the pair to rob the bank. He swore he didn't know how they got there! Tobi knew enough not to acknowledge Patty Long. After all, she was never a friend of his.

Bart was planning how he could escape. A cell mate had given him a homemade knife to hide. When Bart learned via the prison grapevine Patty had made it safely to Canada, Bart hoped there was some way he could do that too. It might be risky, but he wanted to try and immediately began thinking of different scenarios. Every minute his mind raced but he could think of nothing foolproof. After all, what did he have to lose? It was a cut and dried situation… he was going to do prison time.

Without a hope in the world for a pardon and Patty up in Canada free as a bird with several thousand bank dollars to spend, the more he thought about how urgently he must escape. Bart never confided in anybody but he plotted all day and night how he could escape. He would need a car, that was certain. How could he get one?

Suddenly fate seemed to hand him a life-saver! Bart was informed his mother had taken ill suddenly and was in the local hospital fighting for her survival. An appendix had burst suddenly with an infection. She had ignored taking care of herself because she needed to work. By neglecting her health, she really had endangered her life and was now trying to survive.

The prison preacher asked for permission to take Bart to the hospital to visit his mother along with a prison guard. The way Bart saw it, using the visit to his mother was his only chance to escape. It might look callous to others but, Bart thought his mother would understand.

Since his court appearance was not over, they let Bart wear his own street clothes for the visit. When they drove up to the hospital entrance, the minister was waiting inside the door to accompany them to his mother's room.

Bart stuck the sharp knife in the deputies' artery, pushed him down on the ground, grabbed his keys and pistol, and drove off in the police car.

In his mind, all Bart was thinking *"Canada, here I come!"* He was giddy with freedom in his grasp. He needed money first, so he drove to his mother's home and picked up what little cash she had saved in her cookie jar. It wasn't much, but would help him get to Canada.

He exchanged the police car by walking to Tobi's garage and hot wiring his van. Now he was on his way to Canada to see how Patty was doing. It was nice the news at the jail was passed around so freely.

Bart had a location of a town Patty was living in if not her full address. He would fish around in the place and eventually find her.

The only job she was capable of would be waitressing or cleaning. The fact that his escape had been so easy did not worry Bart. His main aim was finding Patty and sharing her part of the bank heist. Vainly, he thought Patty would be glad to see him. Running away to Canada had been real smart!

He never thought she might be running away from him, maybe to start a new life without crime. Bart had always been a bad influence and he was never going to change. Bart had never introduced Patty to his mother and that was a sign she was so insignificant she would never be permanent in his plans. Now that Patty had money, that made the difference in his plans. He always wanted to share in others' good fortunes.

The Kingfisher police captain was sorry Bart had played right into his hands. He knew it was risky to let the man visit his ailing mother, but he gave him the benefit of a doubt and arranged the hospital visit.

However, he himself had been tailing Bart all the way to the hospital then to his mother's home then to Tobi's car. Bart was so predictable the captain knew exactly where Bart was headed. The car and tag license was sent to Canadian police in Toronto. Even pictures of Bart and Patty were provided.

The game was over before it even started for Bart! The Canadian officials were instructed to let Bart find Patty and make the connection before arresting them both for extradition. If Bart had been really wise he would have found a low paying laborers job and settled down staying far away from Patty Long for years. Bart's vision only consisted of getting part of the $20,000 in Patty's possession.

Nothing beyond that thought ever entered his mind. The only thing that did enter his mind was how easy it had been to escape and how providential his mother's appendectomy operation had been.

He did love his mom, but he knew she needed the hospital care and he was not smart enough to help her recover. She was better with him out of her life.

Canada here I come, Bart thought to himself.

Tobi's car was well maintained and full of gas. *It was one good point in his favor. He is a good mechanic,* Bart thought to himself and he was thankful for that little point.

Bart wondered what kind of car Patty Long had bought. She didn't know the first thing about taking care of an engine. Bart's opinion was low for Patty's ability to survive, however she had been smart enough to stay away from all his trouble.

The miles trickled by and Bart realized he was getting hungry. He needed to stop and stretch a bit. He wondered if the stolen car had been put on the internet yet, but hoped it had not. Bart didn't want to be forced to abandon Tobi's car for another one.

What was the risk of entering Canada in a stolen car, he wondered. *Maybe I should stop and buy a bus ticket before going to the border. Would this plan be better or should I enter some other way?*

He really did not want to abandon Tobi's prized possession. Bart trusted Tobi would not rat him out for stealing his car. He felt his friend knew he would take good care of it, so he decided to travel on to Toronto. He really didn't want to travel on foot now that he was getting so close.

Bart slept in the car at night then shaved in a gas station bathroom. He never wanted to look or smell unkempt. His shaving kit accompanied him everywhere along with towel and washcloth. Tobi had never unpacked anything from his car since the trip to Warika Park and there were still things in it Bart could use. Bart didn't think Tobi would be mad at him for using all the comforts of his borrowed car. Friends always shared.

It might take a while to track Patty down, but Bart was confident he could find some kind of employment while he looked for her. He ran over his options in his mind. First, buy a newspaper, check for jobs available. Maybe temporary employment would be easier to find with no questions asked. Washing dishes in a diner did not appeal to him. Hard labor of brick laying did not either.

What could I really do well? he wondered.

Patty heard via newspaper reports from Oklahoma that Bart had made an escape from custody while supposedly visiting his mother. That was just like Bart! All heart, to use his sick mom as an excuse to escape! Patty knew he would consider the money she had to be a prime target and she only hoped he would get caught before he came north for it.

She had no illusions that Bart had any feeling for anyone but himself. Still the thought of Bart being loose was unsettling for her peace of mind. She became extra cautious and more nervous every day.

Patty worked hard at her waitressing job. She helped clean and mop the floors each night before going home, too. Waitressing was hard labor but, very rewarding if done right. Customers were very generous with extra tips if they were well-served and liked the food.

So Patty had been able to save a little extra without bothering from the bank money. The car was the only thing she had purchased with the bank money. She had really needed to get away from all the news going on in Oklahoma to start a new life.

She didn't have any bad feelings for Bart, but she just didn't ever want to see him again or be made to share the money with him.

Chapter 12

Everything was dark when she opened her eyes. Her head hurt all over, especially her face. It was raining and everything was damp. There were night sounds of faraway motors and running water. A headache was something she did not need. She could hear crickets chirping close by.

Must be outside, she thought, but still warm weather for the crickets to chirp. Need to sleep now, she decided, and get some strength. Suzanne slid back into total oblivion.

"Where am I?" Suzanne woke up suddenly.

It was quiet and quite pleasant, the place she lay. A comfortable bed and pillow. Someone was holding her wrist, taking her pulse measurements.

Was she a nurse? What was she doing the pulse thing for? Suzanne wondered.

Everything was muted and quiet and she was tempted to go back to sleep again. Suzanne heard a cart rolling by the door and smelled food.

It must be a hospital, but what was she doing lying in a hospital bed? Fuzzy, fuzzy, dreamy thoughts. *I've just lost my mind,* she decided. *I've been on some other planet and now I'm here, but where am I? The light in the hall was dim so it must be night or very early morning. How did I get here? This must be a hospital room, but I don't know why I'm in it.*

Suzanne's head ached and her nose was sore and bandaged up. She carefully felt her head and face all over. A tube was in her throat too, why?

The nurse saw Suzanne open her eyes and feel around her face. "Good morning, Miss. I'm the night nurse, Carrie Gentry. How do you feel this morning? Doctor Howard will be in soon to see you in a minute, Miss Majors."

"Where am I?" Suzanne croaked.

"St. Jo's Hospital, Miss Majors" the nurse replied. "This is Kingfisher's hospital."

That was a lot of information to think about and it was too early in the morning, Suzanne thought. "I hurt, can you help me?" she asked faintly.

Just at that moment Doctor Howard entered and picked up a pad at the end of her bed. "How are we this morning, Miss Majors? I see you are already awake."

He turned to the nurse and began giving her instructions about food and drink as he quickly retracted a tube out of Suzanne's mouth and throat.

"We will see about getting some breakfast and nourishment in for you, Miss Majors. You have been resting for a few days after your accident."

With that said, he left her room to give food instructions to the nurse at the hall desk. Suzanne wanted more information, so she thought maybe the nurse would help. She felt better with those tubes out of her nose.

Anyway she was too woosey from all the medication she just closed her eyes to rest. Someone was going to have to tell her what happened and why she was here. Her thought were so fuzzy. She did not remember how she arrived at Kingfisher.

Maybe I never arrived and where was Phil's car? Suzanne knew there was a connection to her driving Phil's car home. The puzzling thought was why was she in a Kingfisher hospital? Where was her cell phone? She worried so many questions in her mind – it tired her out and she dozed off again.

The questions kept going round and round and over and over. She was hungry when she woke up again. Someone was urging her to try chicken broth. It didn't taste as good with no salt or pepper in it, but that didn't matter. She was hungry. A few sips of water through a straw were also good.

There was not quite so much pain, just a dull ache. This she could handle – a little less pain and a little more chicken broth. Each sip was a milestone. The nurse told Suzanne the next morning she was supposed to get up, get in the shower and take a bath.

Suzanne was feeling so weak from lying in bed all week long, she thought it was tremendous persecution. Grumbling all the way, she stood while two attendants helped her stand up from the comfortable hospital bed. The whole room whirled around and around in her head before finally settling down.

The rush of blood from her head to her feet left her totally without vision for a second, but the two nurses holding her up steadied her on her feet. It really felt good to be ambulatory again and they helped her walk to the shower. The shower felt wonderful.

Suzanne thought, *I must regain strength and get back home to my real life.*

The second day she was fed real nourishing foods for breakfast, lunch, and supper, plus a vitamin drink which really tasted wonderful. Her stomach was ready for nourishment!

Phil and Frankie were driving back from Northern California to pick Suzanne up. It had taken an extra ten days before the police could find them on their vacation. At first when found at the scene of her wreck, Suzanne was not identified because the car did not belong to her.

They found Phil's phone number from the children living in Riverside that put them in contact. Phil identified his sister as being the driver of his car. Phil and Frankie were advised to be careful driving home and not worry because the Kingfisher doctors were taking good care of his sister. They did not want to create panic and cause another car wreck.

Suzanne remembered her dream vividly. It had seemed so real as she was living in it she wondered if any part of the dream was real.

The sad part of waking up was the absence of Benny Jo, the little dachshund dog. It seemed so funny to miss a dream dog and Suzanne wondered if she could find a real dog to replace Benny Jo.

Suzanne got the Kingfisher newspaper and scanned it avidly looking for any clue about a bank robbery. None appeared and the court cases listed nothing she could connect to. She did not have her cell phone and had seemed to lose everything in the car wreck.

She asked Carey Gentry, the nurse, if she had any clothes to wear home. They had been washed, jeans and tee shirt plus underwear, and were hanging in her closet. Suzanne decided to get dressed in her own things and wait for Phil and Frankie to arrive.

She looked up the address of the humane society and dog pound so she could get Phil to drive over and inspect it. You could never guess what kind of animals resided in the dog pound but, it wouldn't hurt to look. Surely he would not mind taking her to investigate the pound.

Three good meals had given her a lot of strength back, but she was still kind of weak and didn't trust her ankles. Her medication kept her free from most pain.

Suzanne didn't want to become addicted to pain pills or the sleeping pills, so she quit taking them. Actually it was up to her to determine what pain she could handle. If she couldn't get to sleep that night, she would take one pill, but she was not going to be dependent on them! Phil and Frankie took three days of careful driving to get back to Kingfisher at the advice of the police captain.

Suzanne was afraid to look at her face in the bathroom mirror for fear that she had destroyed her nose completely. The nurse assured her she was healing nicely, but she didn't want to see two black eyes and a bandaged nose. The doctor told her she was making him feel bad by not looking at her face. He thought he had done a pretty good job fixing her up. Suzanne thanked him for being so careful and assuring but kept her eyes away from the mirror at each shower.

In her dreams each night, she heard a little dog crying and when she woke she had a feeling of missing someone dreadfully.

Could she have bonded with a little dream dog? Susanne wondered. *Or is there one little pound pup that needed a home with her?*

She just couldn't let go of the feeling someone needed her care. Suzanne began to worry about replacing Frankie and Phil's car. She still could not understand why she had blacked out so suddenly. It was broad daylight when she started home from Enid.

Granting the fact she had turned the wrong direction on the highway and drove south it was still a mystery of what put her to sleep so suddenly. These facts kept going over in her mind.

The wild nightmare dream that accompanied her accident was a puzzle because she never had long nightmare dreams before. She asked Nurse Gentry about the dreams and found there was a court case up against the car manufacturers of her car because the gas fumes were prone to invade the interior of the cars. The fault was in their engineering.

This was a frightful thought. If someone travelled too long on the road the car filled up with enough carbon monoxide it put the driver to sleep. This was the first time she had ever heard of those kind of flaws in a car. She would need to check with her mechanic at home about her own little car.

No one had ever warned Suzanne of her car's engineering flaw before! Being lost in Oklahoma had cost several hours in the car that she had not anticipated. What if Phil and Frankie had driven the car to California instead of buying a new one? They might have been in the mountains when an accident in the car would have been fatal!

This thought really shook Suzanne up. She was thankful to be driving in a good old flat mid-western state when her accident occurred. She decided to have Phil fight that battle out for her. She was not going to be labelled a dumb woman driver! She would come out fighting for her rights!

Suzanne told Doctor Howard of her plans and asked him for all the pictures and x-rays he had of her facial wounds because she felt she was entitled to this proof. There was a bit of pain and damage done to her own health and she felt the car manufacturer should own up to their mistake. This pain was real!

The only good thought she had was maybe Phil and Frankie had been saved from death of plunging off a high mountain top road! She listened to all the Oklahoma news reports.

The hospital had moved her room from the intensive care section to a normal hospital convalescent care room. She would miss the good nurse she had made friends with, Carrie Gentry.

Carrie had given her all the information she knew about her car accident and filled her in on local news. She brought her the Kingfisher newspaper. People here were so kind to one another it made the hospital visit seem friendly and not so scary.

A preacher even came in one afternoon and asked if there was anything he could do to make her feel better.

In her recent dream she had imagined a preacher visiting the prisoner in jail, but she had never thought of one going to the hospital!

It was really the place people would need the comfort of a spiritual blessing more than any place else, she thought.

The preacher had a brought a small gift of hand cream in a little tube for her, with a Bible verse attached. Oklahoma had the heart and art of sharing friendship with all the needy people they came across. She might have to check out all the programs at home to see for herself what Kansas people were doing along this line.

She asked the preacher if he would allow her to visit the different rooms with him to see how he was received by others.

"I know I look pretty awful with all these black eyes and broken nose, Reverend. Do you think I would scare everyone?" she asked.

"I think it would be a good thing and you wouldn't bother anyone at all," he replied.

She accompanied him to the few rooms on her floor and was amazed at the good reception the preacher received by each one. Every face lit up when he knocked at their door to be admitted.

Everyone received a different small gift remembrance. The time in each room was not long enough to tire the person out but, just to be remembered and blessed for the days healing rest. When Suzanne settled back in her own room an hour later, she was tired and ready for a nap. Her brother and sister would arrive the next day.

Then they would start home. Suzanne hoped she could get Phil to drive to the dog pound animal shelter to look for a pet. The little pet she had in mind had long ears and brown eyes of a little dachshund. Her nose felt tight so she knew the bones were healing.

No one in the other hospital rooms had gasped in fright when they saw her enter with the preacher. So she thought her black eyes must be healing too. The doctor wanted to take the dressing out of her nose before she went home. Also, he wanted to see if his stitches were holding in place.

Phil called Suzanne and gave her an idea what time he and Frankie would arrive the next day. He wanted to hear all about the wreck when she was feeling better and did not want to tire her out. The miserable thought that gas fumes from his own car had caused all her misery made him very sorry. Suzanne told him she was glad his new car carried them both safely home and he would not be in any danger. She hoped they would have lots of good pictures to share from the Redwood Forest up north.

California had a lot to offer tourists, especially the Pacific Ocean. The proper way to visit California was to drive from the bottom line of the state up to the northern boundary, with side trips along the way. There should be lots of swimming and eating their different cuisine, from Mexican through Japanese meals.

One restaurant served only meatless hamburgers made of tofu. What a thought.

Her brother tried a Japanese food cafeteria but ate only a salad of green stuff. Nothing else appealed to him. It was kelp he found out later. The cafeteria attendant never batted an eye at his choice of lunch.

Phil and Frankie were really funny as they narrated their spoofy blunders made at each new experience but, the green kelp meal was the best laugh she had all day.

Suzanne told them of her desire to visit the local animal shelter to find a dog companion. They both thought it was a very good idea - someone to take care of and have for a companion. Dogs like to play and take walks every day.

Phil found the address for the animal shelter, loaded Suzanne and Frankie up, and off they went to visit the dog pound. Suzanne was disappointed there were no dachshund breeds available but, all the dogs were well-groomed and trimmed.

Frankie suggested maybe they would find a proper bond at the Ark City animal shelter. So they went to a restaurant for a real meat burger lunch before starting back north up the Chisholm Trail Highway 81.

Maybe there would be a little dog waiting in another city for her. Suzanne was confident she would find a dog like Benny Jo somewhere, sometime.

She coerced Phil and Frankie into visiting the animal shelter in Enid, Oklahoma but, no luck there. Most of the pets had been farmed out to homes for a while. Still, Phil decided to drive over to Ponca City, Oklahoma and visit their animal shelter.

It was on the way back to Arkansas City anyway, he thought. It would please his sister to investigate everywhere she could possibly find a little dog who needed a home. They would leave no stone unturned. Suzanne left her phone and address at each animal shelter they visited.

Any information would be helpful, she thought.

Ponca City had a nice animal shelter but, yielded no dachshund breed. It was a sad thought that she might never replace her dream dog, but she still remained hopeful.

Newkirk was having their weekly garage sale the day they drove up to the Kansas Oklahoma state line - right on the main highway.

It was with a quick look they all saw the little dachshund puppies in the clothes basket setting near the curb to attract dog lovers to stop. These puppies were not in a dog pound. The owners had three adorable dachshunds, but not properly registered show dogs.

One brown, one black, and one black, brown, white three-colored funny looking dachshund but, distinctly fashioned for that breed. All were female, except for the funny three-colored dachshund, and all had beautiful eyes and long ears.

"Well," Phil said "here you get the pick of the litter and every color is available."

There was no hesitation from Suzanne. "Oh, I want all three of them, no doubt about it. They can all play together and keep each other company. I don't intend to separate them, they are a real family," she said.

"It will be expensive to get them spayed and have shots, you know, and all the upkeep for one dog. You'll have to multiply that by three." Phil was amazed.

"I wouldn't want to separate a little family, and there are only three little ones in this family, Phil," she replied.

The deal was set. The owner was glad to have the whole brood taken together because they all loved to wrestle and play together. He made it a good deal for the price, too. It seemed to Phil she was taking on a lot of responsibility, but if that made her feel better, he was glad.

"It's a good thing you have a nice fenced in yard for this family you're taking on, Sis." Phil laughed.

"Oh you! And all the exercise, medications and expense will be triple, but worth it."

Suzanne was anxious to get the little brood home. She had no accommodations for them as yet, and that would be another big expense but, Suzanne was determined. She could make this little brood feel happy and at home.

The shots and the spaying operations would come next with a lot of recovering but, they would have long healthier lives to live and be a great treasure to her.

Names, she thought! *What will be their names?*

Each one had different colored fur but, she was not going to let color influence their names. She would have to study their personalities for clues.

"Could one of them be Benny Jo?" she wondered aloud.

Phil looked at his sister, "Who is Benny Jo? Am I missing some facts here?"

"No, no, I just thought I might name the little brown pup Benny Jo," Susanne said. "I liked that name for my dream dog."

Then she saw a familiar sign: *Welcome to Kansas.* Now we are home! Only one more river to cross!

Epilogue

Suzanne was very tired after her long ride home from Kingfisher, Oklahoma and needed a rest very badly. First she fed all three dogs then took them out back for a little run in the fenced yard. It was good to be back home and on the mend.

She finally got the nerve to face herself in the mirror. The healing of her nose went well and all bandages had been taken off. For that she was very thankful. The fact her face was almost back to normal, if not quite perfect, was a blessing.

While the three dogs raced around discovering their new backyard, she decided to open her mail. In the three weeks she had been gone, quite a lot had accumulated. It was always fun to read all the news in the newspaper as well as the funnies, plus there was a wealth of crossword puzzles in them. Suzanne really liked the puzzles.

Lo and behold, one story contained information about Hastings, Oklahoma and a section sent an invitation to all barn dance lovers with news of a family-friendly barn dance on Saturday night, 7:00 p.m. Bring your own lawn chair, but refreshments would be served by the local Hastings church association.

Kansas families were especially welcome to come and join the fun. Kingfisher central provided the band featuring all the good music for a fun night.

Come one, come all to Hastings 4H Farm for the barn line dance the Fourth of July - an old fashioned Harvest Festival featuring Travis and Heather and the Kingfisher Central Band.

61056175R00083

Made in the USA
Charleston, SC
13 September 2016